A Misstep of Fate

CONTENTS

For my Aunty Susie.
Thank you for always being one of my biggest supporters & for
all that you do. I hope you like this one.
I love you.

Content Warning

Readers should be advised that in this romance and love story there is mention of a gunshot and gunshot wound. I do not go into graphic detail but it does happen on the page. If this is something you are uncomfortable with please read with caution.

Prologue
Bash

Fifteen Years Old

"I do not like it."

"You haven't even done it yet. How can you know?"

"The idea of being paraded around in front of the Queen. In front of the ton. It's ... it's ..." Tilly shakes her head back and forth, her hair loosening with each movement.

"Prescott, are you lost for words?" I smile, glancing at her.

She scowls at me and turns her gaze back to the sky.

Members of the ton stroll along the riverbank. Chatter floats in the air with the light breeze. Children play games on the grass and ladies hold parasoles above their heads to keep the sun off their faces. A few carriages roll past and the clicking of hooves on pavement fade the further they move away from us.

Behind us, our parents sit under a canopy being served afternoon tea and biscuits. My friends are a few feet away smiling at two girls as they make it their mission to make as many of them blush as they can.

Tilly and I lay stretched out on a blanket, grass beneath us and the bluest of skies about. I tuck a hand behind my head as I turn, staring at her profile.

I've never noticed the curve in her nose before. Or how her lip bows. Or the soft angle of her jaw line.

"Bash?" She says and I realise she has been speaking to me. Her eyes turn toward mine and I'm instantly sucked in. The green swirls and shifts in the sunlight. God, she's beautiful.

"Uh," I struggle, the words catching in my throat.

"Who's lost for words now, huh?" She smiles and my heart pounds against my chest.

Chapter One
Tilly

"Oft." The cords crossed into my corset cinch tighter. My hands tighten on one of the wooden posts of my bed as our housekeeper, Mrs Baggins, tugs at them again. The bed shakes and my knuckles are almost white.

God, I hate this.

"Could you be a little gentler? I can hardly breathe," I cough.

"Aye, Mistress." Baggins ties off the cords, pulling a petticoat over my head and fastening it at my back. I'm still getting used to the weight of so many layers of clothing one is forced to wear at an evening event. I shift my balance and glare at Baggins over my shoulder.

"Now. Don't be running around with the Pembroke girl tonight. Your mother has given strict instructions that you must dance with at least four eligible gentlemen," Baggins says in her thick Scottish accent.

"Yes, yes. I know." I spin raising my arms again to allow her to pull the silk fabric of my dress over my head. She smooths down the silk and then pulls out a few curls that catch in the fabric, putting them over my shoulder. Threading her fingers through my long, auburn hair she recites my mother's words from earlier today.

"You're out in society now. You need to find a husband. A respectable match … like your sister," Baggins snorts but she does her best to cover it with a cough. Baggins isn't the only one who isn't all that impressed with my sister or her husband. She tugs at the fabric hugging my body and picks at a piece of lingering lint. "There. Now you're ready to find your *respectable match*."

"Not sure why they insist on the charade. It is quite obvious that they've decided my fate without my input regardless," I sigh. "I heard them talking in the entryway a few days ago. Father's voice carries."

"You mustn't think that way, Mistress." Baggins guides me to sit at the dressing table, adding a few pins to my already styled and secured hair. "Things can change with the right offer," she says quietly, doing her best to reassure me.

The right offer.

I mull the words over in my mind as Baggins fusses with my hair. The only offer that comes to mind is one from Sebastian Archibald. Bash to his friends.

My Bash.

I look up at my ageing housekeeper. She has always been fond of Bash. Even when we were little, she would purposely organise our walks in the park at the same time as the Archibald's housekeeper so that we could play. As our parents became more acquainted, the playdates turned into visits to the summer houses and eventually to the country estates. My family have been regular guests at the Archibald's country home for the holidays over the last few years. Bash and I are friends. Good friends.

More than friends?

Who knows.

The point is that Baggins is fond of Bash. In return, Bash is fond of Baggins.

He flatters her during every visit with his charming smile and quick wit; often matching her Scottish accent and jokingly asking her to make an honest man out of him.

Baggins is the one that ensures Bash's letters make it to me before my father sees them—not that the Earl would have minded all that much in the past, having taken to Bash's charm just as everyone else has in society. Things have changed in the last months.

And I will not lie. As we have grown older, the frequency of our exchanging of letters has become borderline indecent.

I have no doubt that the right offer to which Baggins refers to is an offer of marriage from Sebastian Archibald himself. I am terrified that even that—an offer from the future Lord Archibald, Duke of Wescombe—won't be enough to derail the agreement my father seems to have made already even months prior to my coming out in society.

I turn my head, eyeing the dressing table mirror that reflects the emerald silk that sits tight against my body.

"You outdid yourself with this, Baggins. Truly," I say, running my fingers over the pearls threaded into the corset. "The colour is exquisite."

"You are kind, Mistress." Baggins sets out the matching ribbon that I'll tie around my neck. "I'll take my leave."

"Thank you, Baggins."

The door clicks closed behind the woman as she leaves the room. I sit at the dressing table eyeing my own reflection, my gaze roaming over to the rouge that's lightly dusted across my cheeks. Over the loose curls that fall across my shoulders, the curve of my breasts pressed tightly into my corset.

I force myself to take a deep breath in just to let the air escape slowly, working hard to steady my own nerves and stop my head from spinning. How I long to cut the cords to my corset, strip the stockings from my legs, free myself from the rigid fabric that prevents my chest from rising and falling as it pleases with the rhythm of my breathing.

There's a knock on the door, a pause and then another. I sigh, a small smile tugging at my lips. How they get away with this, I will never know.

"You can come in," I say as the door pushes open, just slightly, and a head pokes around the corner.

Cassius Montgomery's eyes are covered with a hand, his long dark hair tied at his neck, but his devilish grin bares his teeth anyway.

"You may uncover your eyes, Lord Montgomery," I say with a laugh. His fingers part and stormy, grey eyes peer through the gaps. "How did you get up here?"

"It's clear," he says over his shoulder while pushing the door open with more force than necessary to allow the rest of his companions to follow him into the room.

Cassius is actually Lord Cassius Montgomery. His tall frame and long hair, normally wild and free, make the Mamas of the ton both nervous and competitive. His parents passed when he was only fourteen and last year, when he came of age, he inherited his title. Cass doesn't speak much about his family but I know that even before his parents passed away, he spent most of his time residing under the Archibald's roof rather than his own.

Cass wastes no time in stretching out on my bed, his long frame settling amongst the pillows.

Vivi is next through the door. She smiles brightly at me as she skips across my bedroom to sit beside me. The youngest daughter of the Marquess of Pembroke and my best friend, Vivienne Pembroke, is grace personified. Her blonde hair is intricately pinned on top of her head and her piercing blue eyes shine so brightly it almost hurts to look directly into them. Vivi laces her fingers through mine and drops a kiss onto my cheek.

"Hi Tils. I love this colour," she says, stroking a gentle finger over the beading of the front of the dress.

"Baggins made this one," I reply.

"Urgh," Vivi groans. "You're so lucky you have such a talent-ed housekeeper. Coopers is awful at dressmaking. And she's a busy body."

Cassius snorts from his place on the bed.

"Cassius, get your boots off her bed," Frederick Howard says as he leans against the window, eyeing the proceedings in the courtyard below. A few inches shorter than Cassius with short blonde hair, Freddy is one of my favourite people. He's kind and sensitive. A kindred spirit. He will often sneak books to me that I would never be allowed to read and he asks my opinion on issues my father would kneel over if he heard me talking about.

Freddy is the son of a general in the Royal Army who has been fighting abroad for as long as any of us can remember. His father and Lord Archibald were good friends in school so when Freddy's mother died when he was twelve he moved in with the Archibalds. He's been with them ever since.

Bash is the last through the door, shutting it behind him and throwing a wink my way when he catches me staring at him. He crosses the room to join Cassius on my bed. My heart thunders in my chest, pounding so loudly that if it weren't for Cassius' rambling and Vivienne's laughing, I'm sure Bash would hear it from his place across the room.

We all grew up together. Our families have been dragging us to London for the season for years and subsequently, we have been thrown together as our parents play their various roles in society.

"Nothing like a ball on a hot summer's eve to get Freddy scolding like an old man," Cassius laughs, throwing a pillow in Freddy's direction. Vivienne giggles into her hand, causing my eyes to roll and I bump my shoulder against hers. She finds everything Cassius says funny.

I eye Bash stretching out on my bed with his hands behind his head. He looks at me, his hazel eyes roaming over my body. I shift in my seat and feel the heat rise in my cheeks.

"You both look lovely," Bash says. He's speaking to both Vivi and I although his eyes remain firmly on me. Cassius and Freddy turn their attention our way as Bash continues. "How many gentlemen have your mothers insisted you take a turn around the dance floor with tonight? Eight? Nine?"

"Five," Vivi groans.

"Four," I say. "She's actually been quite calm about the whole thing. Although, she had Baggins remind me to ensure I'm on the lookout for a husband just like Florence's."

"Ah, out of luck lads. We're far too handsome," Cassius cries from his place against my pillows. I watch Bash's hand twitch before he runs it through his hair, doing what he can to keep it neat.

I wish he wouldn't.

I very much prefer his messy hair and I very much dream of running my own hands through it. But, that is very much *only* a dream so I return my attention back to Cass.

"Ah but you have the perfect sized ego," I say.

"You wound me, Prescott." Cass throws a hand over his heart.

"Impossible, Montgomery. You are never that easy." Cass laughs at me, Bash and Freddy joining in. Vivi pinches my elbow, asking for my attention.

"What?" I whisper.

"You mustn't tease." Vivi lowers her voice, tilting her head towards mine. "Well, at least you mustn't tease Cass. Bash will get jealous." She nods toward Bash.

"I've no idea what you speak of." I look into the mirror, tucking a curl behind my ear. Vivi pinches my elbow. "Stop it, Vivi."

"Are you ever going to tell the poor boy you're in love with him?" Vivi asks. I shake my head, throwing my friend a hard look. This only causes Vivienne to huff in annoyance. My gaze falls back to Bash.

We live across the street from one another. Our housekeepers are as close to best friends as old and grumpy women can be. We played together as children. We were neighbours. Friends.

Then, he and the boys had gone to boarding school and as a young girl, forced to be homeschooled and taught how to make the perfect wife, I was sure that he would forget me.

I convinced myself that the next time I would see Bash would have been across the room at some ball, years later because that is how it always goes in our world.

But against everything I'd ever been taught about men, Bash went completely against the grain. Three weeks after we had said goodbye, when I'd returned to my family's home in the countryside and settled into my lessons, I'd received a letter.

I poured over his hand for hours after it arrived. He detailed the first days of school and how he thought it was awfully dull without me there. I wasted no time in my reply. I asked him to tell me everything, all the way down to the meals they served at supper, because my country life was just as awfully dull and I was in desperate need of entertainment.

Bash did not disappoint.

He wrote about everything, even the boorish details of the colour of his sheets on his dormitory bed, and he never stopped. He became my best friend, my closest confidant, and I'd fallen in love.

Slowly, but much more deeply than I thought possible.

Last summer I watched Bash's mother parade him about the ballroom introducing him to every young, eligible woman in London. Vivi and I had snuck into the masquerade ball that the Pembroke's threw each year. We peaked down from the gallery only for me to have to watch Bash twirl one of the Vance sisters around the room. His hand skimmed her lower back and his smile had been directed only at her. That was the first time I'd felt the unfamiliar heat pool and twist in my stomach, a tightening in my chest. It wasn't an emotion I liked.

Jealousy.

Wishing I was in her place.

"You ladies are in luck. There are three of us so you will only have to step on one or two strangers' toes," Cassius says as he sits up. He knocks Bash's shoulder as he gets off my bed and steps into the middle of the room facing Vivi and I. He bows low and Vivi erupts into a fit of giggles. "At your service, m'ladies."

Vivi gets to her feet, leaving me to muffle my snicker behind my hand.

"Why Lord Black, you flatter me." She fans her face, smiling widely up at him.

Cass grins, stepping forward to encircle Vivi in his arms and spin her around the room. Vivi laughs, throwing her head back and her dress whipping around her ankles.

Bash watches from his place on the bed and I watch Bash. His eyes follow our friends waltzing around the room before landing on me. He smiles at me and I blush.

Dammit.

He has the type of smile that makes the corner of his eyes crinkle and something burns behind the bright hazel of them. Everytime I am on the receiving end of one of his smiles, I go bright red.

I get to my feet, moving to rest against the edge of the bed. My fingers curl around the same post I held onto earlier as Baggins had practically sewed me into my dress.

"Something on your mind?" I ask Bash, my voice quiet so only he can hear me.

His gaze darts over the features of my face, my hair, the collar of my dress and, if I'm not mistaken, my chest. I suck in a sharp breath to try and steady myself. He doesn't look away.

"Never very much going on up here, you know that," he says after a moment. He touches two fingers to his temple and winks at me.

Swoon.

"Be that as it may, you seem ... distracted," I say. Bash's eyes narrow and he watches me closely as I continue. "Are you okay?"

"My mother has gotten ... more insistent lately. She seems to think I had my fun last season and I am to be more serious about finding a wife this year." He lowers his voice but in the corner of my eye, I see Freddy turn his head toward us slightly and focus on our conversation. Eavesdropper.

"More serious? Were you not serious last season?" I ask.

Bash sits up, throwing his legs over the edge of the bed. I glance over my shoulder, watching as Vivi pulls the tie from Cass' hair and starts threading it into different styles, laughing.

My gaze returns to Bash.

"Sometimes," he begins, reaching up to fiddle with one of the ribbons attached to my dress. "I wish I had a sibling or two so my mother could spread her attention amongst us."

"You are welcome to mine any time you please," I joke and my heart skips when he laughs. I brush my fingers over his hand that still toys with the ribbons gently. "Surely she will not force you into a marriage you do not want. Your mother is a force to be reckoned with, that is true. But I've never seen her eyes soften quite like they do when they are looking upon you."

"You've never seen her yell."

I smile down at him, swallowing the ever present desire to card my fingers through his messy hair. Despite my best efforts, a blooming of hope spreads through my chest. He's looking to make someone an offer.

To throw a wedding.

To find a wife.

I cannot help but allow the desire for it to be me, for him to choose me, burn through my veins.

"But," he continues, pulling me out of my thoughts. "They're older, and she insists that I allow her to throw a wedding before she dies."

"That's ... well, if I'm honest, that's slightly morbid."

Bash huffs, a smirk appearing as he nods. "That's what I told her."

"What are you laughing at?" Cassius asks from his place at my dressing table, his hair sitting messily on the top of his head courtesy of Vivi. Bash doesn't turn away, doesn't pull his hand from where it plays with my dress, doesn't make any sort of movement to answer him.

"Bash is telling Tilly the bad news." Freddy's head turns back towards the window. His forehead leans against the glass as he peers down onto the courtyard below. "Lady Archibald is on the warpath to make our Sebastian an honest man."

"Ah, I see." Cassius runs his fingers through his hair, tying the long locks back into their original bun. He spins on the seat, pulling Vivi down next to him and tucking her under his arm.

"It'll be a sad day for all the mothers of London when Eleanor pushes him down the aisle."

Bash rolls his eyes. He turns his hand under mine and brushes his fingers over the skin of my wrist before pulling away from me.

The hope inside me dims a little as he retreats.

"Your parents certainly know how to fill up a ballroom, Prescott," Bash comments, taking a place next to Freddy by the window.

The use of my nickname falling from his lips, in his voice, makes my heart skip and I once again feel my chest tighten. My eyes dart across the room towards the clock above the fireplace.

"We should go down there. My parents are sure to come searching for me if I do not show my face soon enough," I say.

"To the lion's den then." Freddy pushes himself off the wall.

Cassius gets up, holding his hand out to Vivi, allowing her to curl her arm through his and be swept from the room. Freddy hovers just outside the door, using his foot to rest it against the latch.

Not closed, but closed off.

I join Bash at the window, reaching out to rest a hand on his arm. He reacts, turning to face me.

"What are you going to do?" I ask. "Your mother is nothing if not persistent. Although, I must admit, I'm not sure I see the problem. You've never said you're against marriage ..."

He steps into my space, his hand brushing over the corseted waist of my dress. Fingers curl into the silk fabric as he stares down at me.

"I was hoping to start with a dance. If you'll have me," he murmurs. Even through the fabric of my dress, his touch burns.

I raise a brow. "A dance?"

"Generally what people do at these things." He nods toward the window and the bustling of carriages below. "We might possibly even get away with two."

"Positively scandalous."

"Tilly ..."

"Bash?" I tease. My gaze settles on the hand I have resting on his arm. The crisp black of his dress jacket highlights how pale my skin is.

What a silly thing to be thinking about.

I am currently standing so close to the boy—the *man*—I've fallen in love with, and the only thing I can think about is getting a little more sun.

"You're out in society now. You and I ... We ..." he stutters, swallowing hard. I look up at him, fingers tightening on his arm urging him to go on. "I need to tell you something before we go down there. Tilly, I—"

There is a knock against the door and Freddy pushes through. It opens, the two of us jumping apart. A few moments later, to the sound of thundering steps coming down the hall, Mrs Baggins appears in the doorway.

"Mistress! Your mother had been asking for you. Make haste or she's sure to slaughter us both." Mrs Baggins takes no notice of Bash, or his proximity to me, as she shoos us from the room.

CHAPTER TWO
BASH

I WATCH HER.

I always watch her.

I watch her chest rise and fall as she whirls, out of breath, around the room. I watch her cheeks heat up when Cassius leans down to whisper in her ear. Probably a joke that isn't appropriate in such a public setting. I watch her brow furrow as she converses with Freddy on some topic or another, my friend often asking her opinion on something she would normally be chastised by her parents for even having knowledge on.

Most of all, I watch how others watch her.

Matilda Prescott.

My childhood friend. My neighbour. The love of my life.

I know there is no reason to be jealous of my friends. I have listened to their teasing for years about Tilly's ability to pull my gaze, my focus. About how I would fall over myself every time a letter of hers would turn up at school for me.

All through last year I did whatever it took to keep most of the girls at bay. I danced with a few here and there at my mother's insistence. I stuck to girls I'd known my whole life, ones whose families hosted us when I was a child or ones who were already being pursued by suitors. I did my best to play it safe. I even snuck out early from a few balls.

My friends cover for me because they know.

They know my thoughts are completely and utterly filled with Tilly and only Tilly.

The problem is the eligible bachelors who aren't my friends and who don't know. I watch them as they boldly kiss her hand upon greeting and ask for her to accompany them onto the dance floor.

Right in front of me.

I feel the strong urge to challenge each and every one of them to an illegal duel just to get them away from her.

Last season I had been safe in the knowledge Tilly decided to wait, decided to continue spending her nights reading books and staying well away from the society balls and concerts. Away from the suitors vying for her attention. It is all different now.

Now that she's out, now that she too is attending the same balls and concerts, she is being paraded in front of all those who are eligible and ready to marry her.

I hate it.

I really, really hate it.

"Bash," a soft voice chimes as a woman comes to stand next to me. Reluctantly, I tear my eyes from Tilly.

"Mother." Eleanor Archibald holds a glass of champagne out to me and I take it.

"Stop staring at her. You'll burn a hole in the side of her head soon enough."

"I wasn't staring," I lie. My mother snorts, holding her own glass to her lips to cover the unladylike behaviour.

"I see now why my quest to introduce you to the young ladies of London feels fruitless. It seems the young Ms Prescott has turned your head most completely," she comments, taking my place and staring at Tilly.

"We're friends," I recite. The line practiced and preached for years now. I'm not exactly able to pinpoint when it became a lie. At least, when it became a lie for me.

I tip the glass against my lips and swallow the contents in one.

"I believe that as much as I believe your father when he says the cook just happened to make extra biscuits." I refuse to look at my mother, but I also refrain from seeking out Tilly again. It annoys me to no end that my mother is right. Fundamentally so. Next to me, she sighs. "Ask her to dance at least once before you propose."

"Mother." I sound bored, and my eyes roll, but inside my chest my heart thuds aggressively at the thought.

Do I want to marry Matilda Prescott? Yes.

Am I terrified she doesn't feel the same way and will turn me down? Absolutely.

"Do not take that bored tone with me, young man." My mother turns to me, taking the now empty glass from my hand. "I watched you play as children. I watched you fawn over her letters like they were something precious as a teenager. I saw how unhappy you were when she told you about her decision to hold back from coming out for a year. I tried very hard to ignore how you sulked and brooded through the events of last summer's season."

"I get it—"

"I am not done, thank you." She reaches out to brush the curls falling into my eyes. "You have barely known each other as adults for less than a year but I think you loved her when you were little, too. So ask her to dance, at least once, and if she feels as you do, then you have your answer."

My eyes search the crowded ballroom for Tilly again. Drawn to her in time to see Freddy lead her back onto the dance floor for a second time. She is laughing.

She always seems to be laughing.

Her hands are animated and wild, paying no mind to her casual manner as she tells Freddy a story.

I feel my mother's hand on my back, urging me forward.

"Right," I say to no one other than myself. Inhaling sharply, I try to gain the courage to move. My hands suddenly feel sweaty so I run them down my jacket. My pace is slow, trying desperately to keep myself from falling over my own feet.

God, I'm nervous.

Freddy notices me as I get close enough but Tilly doesn't. I am about to reach for her when she looks up. Not because of my presence but because of the other man that steps in front of her.

I would call him a gentleman but that title is too good for him.

Gregory Talbot bows low in front of Tilly. She hesitates in holding her hand out to him.

"Would you do me the honour of this—"

The knot in my stomach tightens as I watch Tilly's shoulders tense. What I do next is instinct. By the look on Freddy's face it isn't proper and I definitely shouldn't.

But I do it anyway.

My hand slides across Tilly's back. My fingers tighten around her waist. I stand behind her and she leans back against me, instinctively away from Talbot.

"I believe you owe me a dance, Ms Prescott," I say in her ear, loud enough so that our audience watching can hear.

She looks up at me, her hand covering mine and nods. The hint of a grateful smile plays on her lips. "I believe you're right."

She steps away from me and I immediately miss the feeling of her weight leaning against my chest. But then she takes my hand and allows me to pull her toward the crowd of others dancing. She steps into me, her hand fitting comfortably in mine, as my arm slides easily around her waist.

"Thank you," Tilly whispers. "I think a dance with Gregory Talbot would have made me lose my dinner."

She dips her head, laughing. God, I love the sound of it.

"At least try to look a little put out. Talbot looks like he wants to kill me where I stand." I twist, spinning her.

"I will do no such thing. He'll only be encouraged." She tightens her grip, digging her fingers into the fabric of my jacket as I spin her once more. "Besides, you did promise me two dances, to bring up my total and appease my overly eager mother."

At the mention of mothers, something in me makes me search out my own. She is still where I left her except now her head is bent closely to Catherine Prescott.

"Don't look now," I whisper dramatically. "But our mothers are swapping secrets."

"That cannot be good." Tilly stretches on her toes and balances herself against me. I shouldn't like the feel of her pressing so close to me and I definitely shouldn't be thinking about what it does to me but as she leans closer, trying to get a glance at our mothers, the sweet rose scent that radiates from her skin blinds my senses.

I shift and lean away from her, trying to escape the intoxicating smell and clear my head.

"They look as if they are conspiring. God, someone should separate them before they attempt to take over England."

"Hey, Prescott. Focus on me." Another twist of my body pulls her further into the crowd of dancers. "I believe I earned this dance."

"We have plenty of dances ahead of us, Archibald. I think you will live if I am a little distracted because our mothers are *plotting*."

"I think you are *severely* underestimating how long I've waited for this."

Her eyes snap back to me, our mothers forgotten, and she looks up into my face. "Bash. What—"

I could be gentle.

I could choose my words more carefully, speak in a little more riddle in order to protect myself from the answer she may give. But, looking down at her, the gold flecks shining amongst the emerald of her eyes, I lose my head.

"I've been in love with you since we were fifteen years old. Perhaps even before that. I have been waiting to dance with you ever since we snuck out of the nursery to watch our parents at these things. Since I learnt how to dance. So if you don't mind, I would appreciate your full attention because after my confession you may never speak to me again."

I stop moving. No one is paying us much attention as we stand in the centre of twirling couples, skirts and coat tails twisting in flurries of expensive fabric and brightly coloured feathers weaved into hair.

"Bash," she whispers. Her fingers graze across my shoulder, the tips brushing against my neck before curling into my hair. "You are an idiot."

"Sorry?"

"I said—'' She eyes the other dancers apprehensively as she takes my hand. Her fingers thread through mine and tug me through the crowd, towards the doors. The hall is dim in an effort to keep the members of society inside the ballroom and not roaming about the house. Tilly drags me along the corridor. I let her, anticipation coursing through me.

She pushes through the third door to the left and closes it after I follow her through. There is no sitting the door carefully on the latch, no friend standing just outside the room. It is just us in a moment that is stolen and hidden away.

"You, Sebastian Archibald, are an idiot."

"Tilly. The door." I point out. She turns, her eyes roaming over the closed door. She smooths her hands over her dress and pushes her curls over her shoulder before turning back to me.

"You'll excuse me if we ignore the rules of society and have a frank conversation," she says boldly.

"Aren't all our conversations frank?" I question.

"You never said anything. You called me your friend."

"You are my friend," I say. Tilly rolls her eyes. "Well, you were."

Tilly takes a step toward me and I instinctively step back. I rest against the desk of the study. It is dark. A single candle that Tilly lit and left by the door burns low, casting shadows across her face.

"Are we still not?" she asks.

"Of course we are. I misspoke."

"And what you said back in the ballroom? Another misstep in your use of the English language?" I almost laugh as I watch her face flush as she works to keep me pinned with a stare.

I do love it when she yells. When she is so passionate about something she can't keep calm. She forgets all about being ladylike and demure, and lets her opinions fly. She did it when we were kids and even more so as we grew up.

"No, I meant what I said," I say calmly. I push off the desk. Despite my hesitation at the closed door, I find her waist. The silk of her dress is cool under my touch.

She leans into me, reaching to smooth the lapel of my dress jacket with her hand.

She is giving me her permission to leave the rules that have been drilled into us at the door.

It is simply the two of us now.

We move at the same time.

Tilly rises on her toes just as I bend my head. My hands lift to either side of her face, fingers brushing against her neck, behind her ear, her cheek. Hers tighten on my jacket, the fabric crushing in her fists.

She pulls me down further.

I kiss her.

Soft and gentle but enough that my whole world shifts.

It isn't monumental. It doesn't completely throw me out of sorts but something does shift. It is as if I have been in the dark with a single candle lit. But as Tilly touches her lips to mine, the world brightens, and she alone brings the light with her.

I have been walking in the shadows, able to hear her, smell her, touch her, but not truly feel her until she sighs, coils her fingers into my hair, and balances herself on her toes against me.

She makes the world shift. She restores the light. She fills the gaps I wasn't even aware I'd been missing.

Tilly pulls away and rests her forehead against mine. I relax under her touch. The tension built up from watching her interact with men that were not me leaving my body completely now that we are alone.

I kiss her again.

"Bash." Her voice is soft, still so close that I can feel her breath on my lips as she speaks. "We can't."

"I know. I know." My fingers stroke her cheek, familiarising myself with the delicate features of her face. "Tils, you have to marry me."

"I have to?" Her eyes are alight with mischief and if I didn't happen to know her better than anyone else, I might have missed the terrified look she quickly works to hide. "You say it as if you will die if I do not. You are so dramatic."

"I think I may die if you do not," I murmur. I like this look on her. Flushed, out of breath, laughing and mischievous. I am gifted another of her laughs and I close my eyes to commit the sound and this moment to memory.

She traces down my jaw, brushing a finger against my lips.

"I want to," she says. I dip my head, kissing her once more. "But Bash, I can't."

"If you're worried about your parents, I will ask them—"

"My father has already promised me to someone else."

Chapter Three
Bash

I groan as the door slams open. The curtains are wrenched apart and the sun bares down at me through the windows of my bedroom. Freddy hovers by the door as Cassius drops into the chair sitting in the corner.

"You cannot stay in bed for the rest of your life, Bash," Cassius drawls.

I burrow deeper into my sheets. I know it's childish, I know it is well past midday, and I know I should be getting up and going about my day. But as I remember the nine venomous words slipping from the woman I love last night, it feels as if my life is over.

After last night, what is the point of getting out of bed?

Sometime in the early hours of that morning—when the cook told me off for drinking all her good brandy and Michaels removed the crystal from the dining room after I'd thrown a few of Mother's plates against an unsuspecting wall—I fell into bed.

My body gave up and the white hot rage that had been coursing through my veins since returning from the Prescott's party finally cooled.

"Piss off, Cassius," I groan.

"So dramatic." I practically hear the eye roll in my best friend's tone.

One of them tugs off the blankets and lets them thump to the floor.

"Come on, Bash." Freddy shakes my now exposed leg. "Not like you to give up so easily."

I sit up, running a hand through my hair. My body aches, feeling bruised and battered with my heart in pieces at my feet.

"She is marrying someone else," I say. The words taste like acid as they spill out of me.

"So you'll get over her. Stay friends." Cassius picks at his nails absentmindedly. "She's not dying, Bash. There will be others. "

"Cass." Freddy's voice is low and dangerous. My hand curls tightly over the edge of the bed.

I narrow my eyes, the anger that simmered down from last night boils again under my skin. I throw my legs over the edge of my bed, striding towards Cassius. Freddy moves with me, stepping between us and pushing back against my chest. He is much too practiced at tempering his friends' outbursts by now.

"Say it again, Montgomery," I growl over Freddy's shoulder.

Cassius stands up. "Forget about Tilly. There'll be others."

I lunge forward, throwing my weight against Freddy. Cassius doesn't flinch.

"What? It's not like you really gave a shit, anyway. Here you are, holed up in bed instead doing anything about it," he goads.

"What do you suggest, Cass?" I say, still fighting against Freddy. "Should I go over there and demand them to change their minds?"

"Yes."

I stop struggling. We stare at each other, Freddy standing between us, eyes flickering back and forth.

Cassius takes a breath, tapping Freddy on his shoulder, standing him down.

"For as long as I ... as we ... can remember, you have pined after this girl. You stayed up all hours of the night writing novels to her while at school. You came home every chance you got even if you weren't sure you'd see her. You have actively avoided every aspect of high society life until the beginning of this season when she came out."

"Cass ..." Freddy warns.

"You are giving up." Cassius pokes a finger into my chest. "The Sebastian Archibald I know would never, *never*, give up on Matilda Prescott."

"What if I can't change their minds?" It is barely a whisper, a deep fear that lay hidden under the anger and the upset and the shock of it all. It is the terrifying truth, because even if I fight for her, even if I stand in front of her father with the biggest diamond I can find, there is still a chance he'll say no. There is a chance I will still lose her. And that—

Well, I'm not sure I'll survive that.

It never occurred to me, as I skirted ballrooms and passed off invitations the year prior, that she would be promised to someone else.

"You have to try, Bash." Cassius nods as Freddy's hand squeezes my shoulder. "You won't ever forgive yourself if you don't at least try."

I huff out a breath and nod, running my fingers through my untamable hair. He's right. He's a prick, but he's right.

"Did you have to provoke him like that?" Freddy asks behind me.

"Yes," Cass replies. "He had to hear it and it's more fun if I get a reaction."

I shake my head and disappear into my dressing room.

Chapter Four
Eleanor

"Eleanor. What a pleasant surprise." The younger woman rises from her seat on the small sofa as I enter the room. Catherine Prescott is one of my closest friends despite being almost fifteen years my junior.

I was older than the other ladies when I had Bash. Harold and I were sure that children weren't on the cards and then one day, they were. My life was about Bash from the moment he was born. Then he went off to school and brought home Freddy and Cassius.

They become my boys. All of them.

We are neighbours with the Prescott's, and natural friends. Even our housekeepers are friends.

"Catherine," I say, taking the seat across from her. "I apologise for imposing with no formal invitation."

"Don't be silly. You're a most welcome surprise at any time. You know that." She waves me off.

I try to smile, yet find it more difficult when I consider my reasoning for dropping in unannounced. Catherine catches my clouded expression and grimaces.

"Ah. Is it safe to assume that Sebastian is also a picture of woefulness today, just as Matilda is? She has yet to rise from her bed."

"Mm. It took both Freddy and Cassius to rouse Bash. Even then it was well past midday." I shake my head, folding my hands in my lap. "Only after he drank one of the cook's bottles of brandy and smashed a few of my good plates."

"Oh dear." Catherine pauses as their housekeeper, Mrs Baggins, enters the room with a tea tray. We wait for the tea to be poured and the biscuits transferred to the small table before speaking again.

"What I gathered from his dramatic mumblings this morning is that it seems that Matilda has been promised in marriage?" I watch Catherine's hand pause mid-air, eyes widening over her tea cup.

My heart sinks.

"Ah." Catherine sits the tea cup down. "She told the boys, then."

"You will have to forgive me for being confused. We have spoken on the topic of Matilda's prospects many times, and I thought ... Well I thought that you and I were on the same page, as they say." I take a sip from the china teacup in my hand.

"Yes. We were. We are." Catherine sighs. She gets to her feet, moving to poke her head out the door of the sitting room before firmly shutting it. Then, she takes the seat next to me.

"Do you mind explaining to me how we can be on the same page about our children being head over heels in love with one another, yet Matilda has been promised to someone that isn't Bash?" I feel a twinge of guilt at the curt question when Catherine flinches slightly. After all, my tone cuts through all the social niceties.

"Jonathan has come to an arrangement with the Sinclair family. At least that is what he tells me. One that I was not aware of until papers were drawn up and signed." Catherine presses her fingers into her forehead, massaging her temple. "They have invested in Jonathan's business. Apparently, to ensure the business stays in the family, Lord Sinclair suggested Elliot and Matilda marry. It seems my husband is the most oblivious man in the world as he believed Matilda would not mind because Florence certainly did not when he did the same with the Durham family."

"Matilda is not Florence."

"I am *well* aware of that." Catherine nods. "The fact she has told me that she hates me for this more than once tells me that quite clearly."

"Bash waited, Catherine. He waited for her." I set down my tea cup, turning to face her fully now. "I tried to push him towards the other girls to see what would happen, to see if this perhaps was simply an infatuation or obsession. I tried to get him to think about other prospects and he avoided them all. He avoided them all because he was waiting for her."

"I know—"

"He waited for her to come out in society, for it to be *polite*. He finally does the actual asking only to be told no. To be told she is promised to another. So now my son is wallowing and I have lost four of my favourite plates." I throw my hands up in defeat.

I really liked those plates.

Taking a calming breath, I wait for a reply. Catherine offers nothing so I continue.

"Mere months ago we sat in this very spot, drinking the same tea, laughing about how foolishly in love our children seem to be. We have half a wedding planned, for God's sake."

"I know." Catherine shakes her head, her voice quiet, "But what am I to do? I get no say in these things. Jonathan made the deal. If he had consulted me, I would have said—"

"Not a thing happens in the Archibald household that I am not aware of."

Catherine's face falls as a flicker of anger blazes behind her eyes. "And, what is the meaning of that?"

I rise to my feet, knowing that Catherine's anger is about to get the better of her.

"I simply meant that perhaps you better take a closer look at what your husband seems to be doing with the family business. The Sinclair family, Catherine, really? Even you must know how corrupt they are," I say, smoothing a hand down my dress.

Catherine rises too, although it is fruitless; she is a head shorter than me, who stands regal and sharp over her.

"If you are suggesting I had anything to do with this ..."

"You are sacrificing Matilda's chance at happiness—"

"You cannot know—"

"Please. Do not try to justify all this by telling yourself that Matilda could be happy with anyone other than Sebastian. You would have to be blind, positively mad to not see it. I may not know your daughter as well as you but I do know my son—" I take a step toward the door, glancing back at Catherine over my shoulder. "I want him to be happy and if Matilda makes him happy, and he does her, then I will do whatever is in power to ensure they end up together."

The air is thick between us as silence settles. I have always considered Catherine one of my closest friends, maybe even family at times. We shared holidays, birthdays, all manner of seasonal events as one family; the Prescotts and the Archibalds. It saddens me that I hadn't seen Sebastian's infatuation for more than just that earlier. Otherwise perhaps ...

Perhaps I could have done something, anything to stop this from happening.

With no reply from Catherine, I turn towards the door, pulling my gloves over my fingers slowly. I let out a deep sigh, one that oozes disappointment and shame as the air shifts around the room. Catherine sniffs, lifting a hand to wipe the wetness that gathers under eyes. I will myself to stop my face from breaking.

Catherine is my friend but Bash is my son.

"El, please." Catherine pushes the tea tray further onto the table, abandoning the cooling liquid completely as she moves around it and toward me. "Matilda is so very different from Florence. And from me, I suppose."

"You've decided to marry her off because she's different?"

"No! No, of course not," Catherine takes a sharp breath, her eyes meeting mine. "Florence wanted to be a mother, not a wife, and it mattered so little to her who she was with. She came to us ... Jonathan and I ... and asked for our help."

My lips flatten into a tight line, controlling the frustration I feel prickling just beneath my skin. Harold always tells me to keep a calm head, that I react adversely in the first instance. I can practically hear his low voice, whispering in my ear to calm myself and to temper the anger he can feel radiating off me. Whispering to keep a cool head.

A simple touch of his hand is all that is necessary to calm me and I deeply wish that he could be here to offer it now.

"Jonathan and I were in an arranged marriage, did you know that? When I was Matilda's age, my mother gave me half a season of dancing in ballrooms and smiling sweetly at other suitors before sending me down the aisle toward Jonathan." There is no missing the tone of sadness that seeps in amongst her words, twisting itself into a picture of an even younger Catherine, alone in a white dress, walking down the aisle. I watch my friend close her eyes, struggling to find strength in the darkness of her own mind. "I am ashamed to say that I did not recognise the signs. I did not see that Matilda is in love with Sebastian. And now it is much too late."

I falter and a deep dislike for high society expectations courses through me.

"Oh. I wasn't aware that you and Jonathan were—"

"I fell in love with Jonathan. Eventually. But it wasn't until much, much later ..."

"When?"

"After Matilda was born. She ... she had him wrapped around her finger in a way Florence never did." A small smile falls across Catherine's lips. "I think it was the red hair, the same shade as his mothers. It wasn't until I saw him with her that I— anyway." Her eyes sweep around the room, avoiding mine, as she blinks away the tears forming. "I am sorry. Of course, I always wanted—"

Without thinking, I move again. Back to the lounge, tugging off my gloves as I sit once more. Pity forms in my stomach and I take a deep breath. It is obvious my friend wasn't privy to the plans that were made for her daughter. My anger is directed at the wrong person. I pick up the small, china teacup and bring it to my lips. The tea is cold now but it's no matter. My eyes follow Catherine as the younger woman slowly, hesitantly, makes her way to sit back down next to me.

"I want her to be happy now. Not in a few years time, not after she has ..."

I smile.

Finally, on the same page.

We will find a solution, we will find a way.

"We best think of something soon then, before my son does something dramatic and completely in character. Such as stealing Matilda away to Gretna Green."

Chapter Five

Bash

"Warm today, is it not?" I pull at the collar of my jacket.

"Uh—"

Tilly's eyes raise toward the sky, an amused smile itching at the sides of her mouth, the smooth skin of her cheek dimpling as she lets out a short laugh.

As I watch her, following the way her neck stretches with such intensity I feel my eyes sting, the heat rises further up my neck. Being around her used to be easy, effortless. But it has changed. I can't remember when exactly things shifted. Being around her now involves my britches tightening and the temperature of my body scorching to ungodly heights. I nervously stumble through words because I can't help focusing on the soft pink of her lips.

I can see the same flush colouring in her features when she glances at me. It lights up her face just as it had nights ago when I held her in my arms, when I kissed her and finally got to really feel the shape of her lips.

"There isn't a blue patch through the clouds and it rained this morning," she says.

"Just me then," I mutter quietly, feeling as if I'm on fire under her gaze. I shove my hands deep into my pockets.

She twists her gloved fingers together, held gently behind her back. I long to reach for them; to be able to add my own to the fray, to hold her hand tightly in mine, to pull her closer to me.

She fits so perfectly, like she is made for me.

Made for me, promised to someone else.

Her words echoed in my head again, taunting and twisting.

My father has already promised me to someone else.

How bloody unfair.

I watch the cobblestone street disappear under my feet as we walk towards Hyde Park. Cassius has Vivienne tucked tightly into his side, arm twisted through hers. They walk in front of Tilly and I, while Freddy wanders behind.

Baggins and Michaels walks even further behind him, chaperoning the five of us from a distance as they have done since we were children.

"You ... are you okay?" Tilly asks quietly. None of the others hear her. I shake my head, glancing across at her. "Bash—"

"Tilly." Vivi whips her head around to look at us. Her voice breaks through the quiet, heavy air that fell around us. "Look, it's that dress you love. We must go and see."

Vivi untangles herself from Cassius, taking Tilly's hand easily in hers before she pulls her across the street.

Of course, my gaze follows her. The swing of her hips, the bounce of her hair, the glance she throws over shoulder with her eyes apologetic and amused at the same time.

I kick a stone along the ground as the other two boys slow to a stop with me.

"So?" Cassius asks expectantly.

"So, what?" I murmur not looking at either of them.

Cass groans and throws his hands out. This earns him a glare from Freddy.

"Come on, Archibald. Get your head right." He pokes my chest.

Freddy places his hand on my shoulder, pulling my attention away from Cass' terrible attempt at a pep-talk. "What I think he is trying to ask is, did you find out who it was?"

A sound floats from across the street, my ears picking it up immediately. It turns my attention toward Tilly.

My whole body moves away from my friends and toward the sound of the laughter that carries across with the wind to me. It's like a magnet pulling us together. Her red hair is tied loosely at her neck but rebellious strands fall over her shoulder in waves. The curls are bright against the dark navy colour of her dress.

My lips tug upward as she twirls around Vivienne, obviously in the midst of passionately proving a point.

"We'll take that as a no," Freddy sighs as he clicks his fingers in front of my eyes. "God, Bash. Stop staring at her like that."

I blink once, then twice, before turning back to Freddy.

"We cannot talk. Not honestly, not here. Tonight at Vance's evening riverside picnic there will be more of a distraction. She and I can talk then." My eyes drift back to her, catching her gaze as the girls make their way back across the street to us.

My heart beats hard in my chest as she settles herself between Freddy and I, threading her arm through mine. She's done this before: when we were children and playing in the gardens, and then again when we were older as we walked behind our parents with our heads bowed together in whispered conversation.

But now with the memory of how it feels to hold her against me, the way her lips move against mine, the feel of her cheek beneath my fingertips still freshly scorched into my mind, having her so effortlessly within reach feels like a twisted sort of torture designed solely for me.

I bend my head towards hers, inhaling the scent of her skin as I hover inches from her ear.

"Can we talk tonight? Alone?" I hesitate, fighting with myself to pull back and not to drop a kiss against her neck instead.

When she nods, I pull away.

"Yes. I— of course we can talk," she replies quietly.

"The Vance's?"

Another nod, my hazel eyes boring into her emerald ones as she searches my face.

"Yes."

The slight crease in her brow paired with the downward tug of her mouth and the signs of a frown appearing on her face makes me swallow hard. I struggle with myself to not immediately lift a thumb to her brow in an attempt to smooth it away or to brush my lips against hers in the hopes she smiles instead.

I'm not able to do anything other than thread her arm more securely through my own.

By God, do I want to do more.

Instead, I smile and look straight ahead at the backs of our friends. I keep my voice quiet when I say, "I can't stop thinking about our kiss."

Immediately the colour of her cheeks turn a deep red, her mouth twitching into a smile as she hushes me. Her hair flicks wildly over her shoulder as she glances behind us at our chaperones following a few steps behind.

"Bash, you mustn't."

"Mustn't, what?" I smirk, looking down at her quickly. "Mustn't kiss you again? Did you not enjoy it?"

"Stop it." She swats at my arm. "You know I—"

"Because if you didn't enjoy it then you must let me try again."

"Must I?" she says playfully.

"You're constantly telling me to give people second chances." I squeeze her arm again.

"You're impossible." Her head drops to rest against my shoulder. It's only for a moment but the easy smile that forms across her lips and successfully chases the frown away feels like a victory.

I reach up with my free hand to tuck a stray strand of hair behind her ear before pulling her a few steps forward to join the others.

It is gentle, soft and brief.

But there is no missing the quiet sigh that escapes her lips at the contact and that alone is enough to set my pulse racing.

Again.

Chapter Six
Tilly

The hem of my soft, cream gown drags a little across the carpet of the corridor as I twist my hands in front of my churning stomach. My nails dig into my palm as I search for the courage to knock against the door to my father's study.

The last time I was in this room, I clung to Bash as his mouth covered mine and his hands burned through the fabric covering my body. My heart races as I remember the way his crisp shirt crumpled in my fists and how he pulled the air from my lungs with his stupidly handsome grin.

I steady my breathing as I think about kissing him again. Heat weaves its way through my body, attaching itself to my nerves and setting my skin alight. I shake my head, trying desperately to clear it.

My father's study is no place for thoughts of Bash, or his mouth, or his hands, or any part of him for that matter.

I need to focus.

I push lightly on the wooden door and refuse to think of the reckless way I shoved Bash into the room a few nights ago. *Focus.*

"Father?"

The room is stifling. The fireplace is lit and burning despite the summer sun heating the windows behind my father's desk. I loved this room as a child. I used to steal away from my lessons to hide by the same window. I would curl onto the small seat with my head resting against the glass as the sun warmed my face.

One of the walls is lined with books, the dusty and the new alike. If I squint, I can still make out the small, torn off pieces of spare parchment that poke from some of the books I'd been particularly fond of back then. With a soft smile crossing my lips, I remember the way I would excitedly scribble my thoughts onto the parchment and slip them between the pages that held words that I'd laughed at or made me cry.

Back then, I had been so sure that whatever book I was reading was going to be my favourite. It had been, until I picked up the next one.

"Tilly? Should you not be getting ready for the Vances' party?" My father looks up from his desk and eyes me curiously.

I smooth my dress down with my hands, fixing him with a feigned look of annoyance. "I am ready. Do you not like it?"

"You always look divine, my darling," he laughs. He smiles fondly at me but I can't help notice the smile doesn't reach his eyes quite like it used to. "Do you need something?"

"I wanted to talk to you about—" My eyes wander the books again, the hundreds of stories I once lost myself in. Back when things were much simpler and Bash was simply the boy across the street.

Bash.

Just the thought of him makes my stomach flutter, the same warmth that I felt when his hand touched mine floods through me as I picture his smile as clear as day in my mind.

The thought spurs me forward.

"I want to talk to you about the marriage arrangement you have made for me."

If my father is surprised that I already know about the marriage arrangement, he barely shows it. His smile tightens, his mouth presses into a firm line and he sits straighter in his chair. A deadly silent moment passes between us. Then he waves for me to sit.

So I do.

I sit.

I stare across at my father, waiting as he takes a thickly rolled cigar from the top drawer of his desk. He concentrates on lighting it, his cheeks hollowing as he takes a deep breath, inhaling.

"It is quite the advantageous match, darling. I do believe you and the young Mr Elliot Sinclair will make a handsome couple," he says, the smoke billowing out of his mouth in the same breath.

My stomach rolls.

"*Elliot* Sinclair? Elliot *Sinclair*?" I stammer and stagger through his name. My throat constricts as my mouth goes dry. "You're marrying me to *Elliot Sinclair*?!"

"He seems like a well educated lad. His family are quite pow-er—"

"He is vulgar, father. He's an awful choice and everyone in the entirety of England knows his family are as dishonourable as they come." I get back to my feet and start pacing, burning holes into the deep red carpeted floors.

Elliot Sinclair?!

I cannot.

I will not.

I listened to Cassius rant and rave about the family for hours once. It was before his parents died and they tried to arrange a match between him and Sinclair's youngest daughter, who was only ten at the time. They would do anything to gain more power, more status within society. That family holds onto their status through money, lying, and cheating.

Elliot Sinclair is a few years older than me but he attended the same school as Bash. Even though Elliot was older, he stood out enough that Bash wrote to me about him. He was a bully.

A bully and a rake.

I hadn't been surprised when Elliot had returned from his studies at the University of Oxford early, claiming to have been bored, but the rumours around town said differently. Expelled, Cassius told us. When I pressed for further details, Cass simply shrugged his shoulders and told me that whatever Sinclair had done, his parents had paid a lot of money to keep it quiet.

To this day, Cass' fist still clenches tightly whenever the older boy gets anywhere near me or, God forbid, Vivi.

"Come now, Matilda. You mustn't listen to trivial gossip from the servants. The Sinclairs are a respected family." My father's eyes, the same deep emerald colour as my own, follow me as I slow my pace. I steady myself by curling a fist around the back of the armchair I vacated.

"Father, please. You can't. *Please.*"

"I am sorry you feel this way. I thought it was quite a decent match for you. I thought you would be pleased."

"What if I have another—" I pause, my tongue tying as the feeling of *his* lips ghost across mine, again.

It feels awfully silly of me to get so flustered at the mere thought of Bash when he has been pulling at my pigtails since we were children.

He crept into my mind, took a seat, and never left.

He is familiar.

So incredibly familiar that I often think I may know him better than myself at times. But, after the kiss, it seems as if my life has split into two. There is the before—when Bash was a written word in a letter or distant laugh from across the grass on which we played—and then the after. He's become soft touches and blazing stares from across ballrooms. His name, the trigger of my most carnal thoughts.

I take a deep breath.

"What if I have another offer? A better offer?" I ask my father.

We stare at each other across his desk. I notice he looks tired. His skin is pale. He seems to be counting the seconds, his eyes searching my face as they dart lazily around my features. I can't help but stiffen under his gaze. He leans forward, elbows resting on the desk, parchment crinkling with his weight.

"I am sorry, my dear. It is done."

"Father—" He jerks forward slightly, holding a cough in his chest as he smothers his mouth with a hand. I pause, stepping forward instantly as if to take hold of him. He waves a hand at me, calling my advancement off.

"I am fine," he splutters. "I'm afraid I've caught a small chill."

"Are you certain?" I tilt my head, my hand twitching like it still wants to reach for him.

He nods. "Yes."

"I—"

"Elliot Sinclair is a decent match. His family is wealthy, highly ranked, and he will inherit a title." My father rises from his seat and moves around the desk. He reaches for me and tucks a stray hair behind my ear. Then, like he would when I was a small girl, he touches a fingertip to my nose lightly. "You will be well taken care of and the business will stay in the family. Besides, the Sinclairs live in London full-time. You love it here. No more suffering with travel when—"

"Florence," I interrupt, the name falling from my lips with disappointment while my throat constricts as I feel a familiar sting build behind my eyes.

My father stops, glancing at me over his shoulder as he gathers his gloves and coat from where they are thrown over a chair. "Excuse me?"

"Florence loves it here," I repeat. "I ... I've always wanted to live in the country."

"Oh." He slides his arms through his coat, muffling another cough into the sleeve. "Well no matter, I'm sure you will learn to love it here."

"Father, please—"

"Now Matilda, none of that." He moves to press a gentle kiss to my forehead, his fingers wrapping around my wrist. "I will be attending the Vances' party tonight. Lord Sinclair agrees that you and Elliot should become acquainted."

"But—" I begin my protests again.

"It will be fine, my darling. I am sure of it. No more talk of others. I will see you later." He shakes my wrist gently as a goodbye.

There is nothing else to do other than allow it, my body numb. When he can't coax anything more from me, he simply sighs and leaves me standing in the study alone.

There is nothing more to say.

If Bash's confession is a brightly painted mural of our future—one of certain happiness filled with laughter, and smiles, and lips pressed against lips for the rest of time—then my father's refusal to listen covers it all with the darkest of dark shades.

It is a black curtain, pulling across the envisioned life.

It is the door to the country house of my dreams, slamming shut with me on one side and Bash on the other.

The door to the study clicks shut just as I fall back into the chair, my fingers gripping tightly to the arms and digging into leather. I will myself to just breathe.

In and then out.

I think I may die if you do not.

The words were said with his stupidly happy grin spread right across his face. There was no ring and no grand gesture. No formal visits and no courting period.

We went about it all wrong, sneaking away like that and I gave in to my better judgement even though I knew, *I knew*, I had to tell him.

I wish I had pushed back sooner. I wished I questioned Father quicker.

Deep down I hoped it had been Bash.

I'd wished for it.

Instead, I ignored the painful choice and let him kiss me.

I gave him permission and then I met him halfway.

But, when he had asked—when he had demanded—for my hand, I got a glimpse of a future that could be and I have never wanted something more in my life.

I wipe the single tear from my cheek, sniffling a little as I get up from the chair. I am about to leave—to face my mother again, maybe demand she do something about this situation because I can't allow the fairytale in my head to die without even trying to save it—when I see the curled signature of my father scribbled harshly next to another.

Glancing at the door, I round the desk. My hand glides lightly over the parchment stacked in unorganised piles. My eyes skim the words.

*This document forms a contract between Mr Jonathan Prescott
and Lord Theodore Sinclair II in which...*
...Lord Sinclair to invest Ten Thousand pounds...
...Prescott Trading & Co...
*...the agreement of youngest daughter, Matilda Catherine
Prescott in marriage...*
*...Prescott Trading & Co to pass first born son of Elliot Sinclair
and Matilda Prescott...*
...to be run by proxy by Elliot Sinclair until of age...
...binding...
...dowry waived with exchange of hands...
*...Country Estate passed to the first born son of Mr and Mrs Victor
Durham...*
...full time residence in London...

I finish reading, and there is no longer any air left in my lungs, or the room, or anywhere. My eyes fall across the other pieces of parchment: a list of house accounts, statements from the business, banking statements, and a half-filled payroll.

"God," I murmur. I finger through the parchment, the rejection letters for bank loans and the employer pay cut notices. My hands shaking and my mind reeling, I tuck one of the rejection letters into the sleeve of my dress.

The sounds of my heavy footsteps are muffled by the carpet as I weave in and out of rooms, out of breath and desperately searching for Baggins.

I find her in one of the upstairs guest rooms, fluffing pillows and keeping herself busy.

"Matilda, my child, you are all flushed. What is it? What has happened?"

"Father, he … I don't understand … The letters, the contract …" Baggins holds a soothing hand on my arm, keeping me steady like she knows that I will sink through the floor from the weight of my heart if she does not. "Bash. I need … Can you send a message to Bash?"

"The Vance picnic is in a few hours. Can you not wait until you see him?"

"Now. I need to speak with him now. I cannot … the Sinclair boy … I have to tell him before …" I shake my head, the pins in my hair loosening violently as the curls fall over my shoulder. Panic seizes my chest and I struggle to breathe. A few tears fall down my cheeks.

"Okay, okay." Baggins pulls me into her chest, holding me tightly as she measures her own breathing for me to mimic. "I will send for him."

***

The pins slide easily back into my hair but I feel it is fruitless, knowing with a restless finger they will just be falling again within minutes. My hands twist on my lap. My thoughts reel as I wait for Bash.

I know he will come. I know he will answer the call.
When has he not?

All through school, there was a new letter weekly. During the summer, every morning without fail, there he stood on my doorstep with his hand outstretched, ready for the day's adventure.

He will come.

There is a knock, a pause, and another knock.

Despite the conversation about to be had, my heart still skips a beat. Still races at knowing who stands on the other side.

I turn the handle, finding his hair as messy as I like to see it. His black waistcoat sits untidily over his shoulders like he rushed getting dressed. Freddy gives me a small, amused smile as he leans on the wall opposite my bedroom door. As Bash enters, brushing past me, his fingers graze my stomach, picking up my hand on his way past and holding it in his.

Freddy waits in the corridor. Not that anyone is likely to come up here. The household staff have been turning a blind eye to Vivi and the boys sneaking in for years.

"You sent for me?" he jokes and my head spins.

His laugh. God, I would miss his laugh.

When I don't return his smile, the same fear I feel deep in my stomach shows on his face. Immediately he crowds me, fingers lifting to brush over my cheeks.

I will myself not to cry. Not yet. Not until he is gone.

"What's happened?" he whispers.

"I ... do not know how to begin. It is—"

"The beginning, always from the beginning," he states. He is so close. So warm as I allow his presence to wrap around me like a comfortable blanket. If I push up onto my toes, I could capture his lips and I long to remind myself, if for the last time, what they feel like.

I sigh and my eyes close under his touch.

"I— My family is broke … I think," I whisper.

His brow furrows. "Pardon?"

"My father." I motion to the open letter I stole from my father's desk, which now rests traitorously on my bed. "He applied for all types of loans and he got declined. For them all."

Bash lets me go, striding over to the letter. His eyes race across the parchment.

"Hasn't this business been in your family for years?" he asks.

"My grandfather was quite the businessman. My father, it seems, is not." I can't help the disappointed tone in which I speak of my father now.

"What has this got to—" Bash looks up at me. Halting when he sees the tears welling in my eyes.

"There was a contract of investment on his desk." I tug at my sleeves as the words roll off my tongue, fast and rehearsed. I practised how I was going to tell Bash but I hadn't counted on my resolve almost breaking the moment he touched me. "The Sinclair family is investing in the business and in exchange, so that it can stay within the Prescott family, father promised me to Elliot. Or, they promised Elliot to me. Regardless—"

"Elliot Sinclair?! Christ." Bash swears.

"It no longer matters who it is, Bash." I swallow hard, my throat dry. "The deal has been done. The money invested, the plans made. I cannot change anything. Not even ... with a better offer."

I look down to study the hem of my dress closely and hide the furious blinking I am doing to avoid the tears. I don't miss Bash's frustrated sigh as the parchment floats into my eyeline, landing on the floor next to my bed.

"What do we do?" He says, disappointment dripping in his tone.

"I have to marry him. My family will be ruined, my father's reputation destroyed, my mother ..."

"There has to be something we can do," he interrupts.

I can tell he is running through all sorts of wild ideas, all probably plausible but none of them possible.

Not anymore.

Not now that it is too late. I look at him, at everything that makes me ridiculously happy—from the messy locks on his head to the swell of his chest that protects the heart I love so dearly with my own—and the tears finally fall. I feel defeated.

Bash wraps me in his arms instantly. My head falls against his chest, tucking beneath his chin as I inhale his scent like it is the only thing keeping me alive now. It is the way my heart tightens and how heavily the tears fall and his automatic reaction to simply needing to hold me that makes this all the more difficult.

I sniff, the most un-lady-like of sounds, but it only makes Bash grip me tighter.

"It is not fair to spend so long loving you but so little time being with you. I wish it were different," I say into his chest.

"So don't. Don't marry him, Tils. Marry me. We can leave. We can just go and they will think us dead or run off or something. The scandal alone would be enough for your family to appear innocent in it all. We can live our lives in the countryside. Just us. Just as you always wanted to."

"And what of your family? You're an only child, Bash. You can't just run away."

"I will send word to them once we are gone. But we will need to be far enough—"

"Always so dramatic." I laugh darkly. He touches a hand to my cheek, wiping away the stray tears. My eyes close under the contact. I think I will miss this the most. "I will not ask you to do that. I will not ask you to give up everything for me."

"I am nothing, I have nothing without you."

Bash kisses me.

He kisses me with more force and more passionately than those we have shared before. I curve into him, fitting against the lines of his body so perfectly that it tears my heart further in two. When he breaks the kiss, I am left heaving as I try to catch my breath and try to clear my head so I can eventually muster the strength I will need to walk away from him.

With a hand on his chest, I push him back and say, "I'm sorry."

"Please, do not do this." Bash palms my cheeks again, tilting my face up to his. I shake my head. My unsteady breaths turn into choked sobs, wrecking through my body as I shake in his arms. "Please, Tils. Please."

There is a knock and Freddy slips inside the room.

"Time to go," he says quietly.

"A moment, Fred. Please," Bash says through gritted teeth. He doesn't let me go.

"You do not—"

"A moment!" he bellows, his eyes finally leaving my face but his grip tightening on my arm.

Freddy moves toward us. His hard gaze flickers between me and Bash before he places a hand on his friend's shoulder. He shoves Bash backward and away from me.

"You do not have a moment. They have other guests arriving. Being caught here will do nothing good for her reputation. Nor yours, for that matter. We will find another way," Freddy says sternly.

Bash doesn't move. He returns Freddy's hard stare, the hazel turning dark and his eyes storming dangerously.

I watch him. The tension in his shoulders, the lines of his face, the fists his fingers have curled into. For the first time ever, I am a little scared of my sweet, kind Bash.

"That is not how you want to do this. We will find another way." Freddy repeats, his voice low and calm but forceful. I turn away from them, desperately trying to muffle the renewed sobs against my hand that I hold to my mouth.

By the time I can bear to look, Freddy has pulled Bash from the room without another word.

Chapter Seven
Eleanor

"The pearls, darling. Always the pearls."

I smile, lifting the pearls to my ears. I can feel him hovering before his hands find me. Fingers gently rest on the curve of my hips and I turn my head, allowing him to place a delicate kiss to my cheek. I sigh, content to simply stand in his arms and enjoy the quiet moment.

Harold Archibald took my breath away the moment I met him. Seven years my senior and a set look of distinct boredom etched on his face, I watched him from afar, sure I'd never do much else. He barely danced with any girls at the balls, let alone courted one.

That was until the day we found ourselves seated next to each other at an Opera performance. It was all sideways smiles and whispered commentary, and by the end of the evening his signature frown was nowhere to be seen.

He arrived at my parents' home the next morning, roses in hand, and asked me to marry him on the spot.

When you know you know, he said to me.

I burst out laughing at the absurdity of it all. I told him to get off his knee and stop being silly. That we'd spoken once the night before and that he couldn't possibly just know.

He asked for my hand a total of five times before I finally said yes.

"Where's our son this evening? I thought he was joining us tonight." Harold asks softly, resting his chin atop my tightly pinned hair.

"Freddy told Michaels they were going for a drink at the club before the party, but I have a feeling he is with Matilda," I sigh.

"Isn't he always?" He laughs. My husband and son have the same laugh. Just as they share a nose, hair, and smile.

"This business with Matilda, Jonathan and Catherine just promising her to someone else without speaking to us, I do not like it," I say quietly. "Not one bit."

"Ellie," Harold chastises. "You mustn't get involved. If Sinclair and Prescott have agreed, then we must stay out of it. Bash will get—"

"Would you have gotten over me?" I interrupt, turning in his arms. He leans down, arms tightening around me and entwining himself with me effortlessly. "Would you have walked away?"

"Well, I—" Harold's brow furrows, "No. No, I could not have walked away."

"Neither will Bash." I reach a hand to his face, fingers caressing his beard shadowed cheek. "You two are too similar for you to truly believe he will simply get over her."

"Do not get involved, Ellie. Sebastian can speak with Jonathan, make an offer of marriage, but if they decline then you must leave it alone."

"I—"

"Eleanor, I mean it. I will not have this family on Sinclair's radar." He grasps my hands in his. "I am serious. The man is dangerous."

I shift my weight, eyes darting around the sitting room. "Fine. I won't do anything to get in Sinclair's way."

"Eleanor." He narrows his eyes.

The vase sitting over the fireplace shakes when the front door slams.

Hard.

Harold and I share a look before making our way into the entrance hall where two bodies are scuffling across the marble floors.

"Boys," I scold, tutting as Harold jumps forward to separate them.

"Let me go, Fred." My son fights off Freddy's hold, pushing the sandy haired boy away from him.

I frown as I watch my son and a man as good as a son glare at each other from across the room. Freddy's father is an old friend of Harold's. He's a general in the army and when Freddy's mother died some years ago, we took him in while his father was away. Freddy spent his teenage years in this house.

Harold stands between the boys.

"Use your brain here, Bash," Freddy hisses. "What was the plan? Knock on the Sinclair's door and what? Kill Elliot on the spot?"

"No. I just—" Sebastian's hands fly to his hair, tearing through it. "I have to do something."

"I know that and I want to help, but you need to be rational about this. What would it look like, huh? Their engagement is not even public knowledge yet." I watch as Freddy pleads with him. "Think about what it would look like if you just tore from the Prescott's and went straight over there. You would put her reputation at risk. You put it at risk just by going there today. I know neither of you want a situation where you get caught and her reputation is ruined. That is not how you want to achieve your goal."

"He's right, son." My husband uses a much softer tone, crossing the short distance to place a hand on Bash's shoulder, anchoring him. "Calm yourself."

Bash steadies his breaths, aligning them with Harold's, and I move to stand next to Freddy. I pick up his wrist and examine the purple patches forming across his knuckles.

"You boys, I swear. You'll be the death of me," I tut.

Freddy offers a quiet apology. "Sorry, Eleanor."

"What happened?" I look over to Bash and ask.

"She ... I cannot ... there is no way out," Bash speaks, eyes still on his father. "Her family are ... they ... Mr Prescott agreed to the marriage in an investment contract. It was all about business. They do not even care that I ... that she—"

"A business contract?" Harold asks, his eyes flying to meet mine. "What are you talking about?"

Bash just shakes his head, words failing him, so I turn back to Freddy with my brows raising in question. "Frederick?"

"I—" Freddy throws a glance at Bash before swallowing. "I didn't really catch all of it and I wasn't really trying to listen, but you were sort of yelling at each other, mate."

I roll my eyes. Typical behaviour of my son and Matilda. Their emotions are so intense when in the presence of one another that it channels into either untapped frustration or overwhelmingly obvious flirting.

I nod at Freddy to continue.

"Lord Sinclair has invested in Mr Prescott's business. He claims to be in some sort of trouble, financially, and in order to ensure that it stays within Prescott's hands, they agreed to an arranged marriage between Tilly and Elliot."

"What does Sinclair know about international trading?" I asked Harold.

Harold just shakes his head, hand still tight on Bash's shoulder.

"More than you think. They bought out the entirety of Ryan and Sons' ships about eight months ago. Had them brought in at Leeds to have them repaired and repainted. If he is going after Prescott's business then it seems he plans on holding the monopoly of England's trading market. If he can," Harold says.

Now I am the one to shake my head. "I cannot believe Jonathan would agree to this."

"I do not expect he knows the whole truth." Harold pulls Bash into a tight hug. "I'm sorry, Bash. I know you felt very strongly for Matilda."

"She does not want to marry him," Bash says. I can see the silent plea behind his words, his eyes boring into Harold's, desperately asking for a solution. "I know she doesn't."

"Her parents have made that choice for her." I let out a low hiss, warning my husband of any further insensitive comments. Harold throws me a look and his eyes flash, warning me.

I, however, am not just another lady of London. I am Eleanor Archibald and I have no problem challenging my husband. I fix him with a similar glare in return, knowing we will likely argue this out when we are alone.

Harold continues anyway, "The only thing left for you to do is make an offer of your own and respect whatever answer you may get."

"They will say no," Bash replies, defeated.

Silence falls over the four of us. Harold pulls Bash back into a hug as my fingers trace over Freddy's hands absentmindedly. Bash pulls back from his father, rubbing the sleeve of his shirt over his face with bloodshot eyes before turning away from us.

Harold sighs, patting his back once more, before he turns to Freddy.

"Your father has written, Fred. Come with me, we need to discuss a few matters," he says quietly as he moves. Freddy throws Bash another look before following Harold dutifully down the hall, towards his study.

I cross to Bash, placing a small hand on his back. I can feel the unsteady breaths he draws.

When I married Harold I had been so young, and so in love, and I had never left England. Harold took me all over the world, pulling me from my day to day duties at a moment's notice because he simply had to show me this country or that.

We never were careful, per say, when it came to preventing children. We were content with just letting it happen whenever it did.

But, years flew by and I never so much as thought I might be pregnant at any time.

When I finally came to the conclusion that it wasn't meant to be for Harold and I, I fell pregnant with Sebastian.

Our miracle.

Harold had been out of his mind with worry, insisting I lift nothing heavier than a cup of tea once the doctor had confirmed I was pregnant. I was in disbelief, even as my stomach grew and my feet swelled, I found myself hesitant to truly believe he was coming.

And then he was born. My focus, my energy, my whole life revolved completely around him and our family of three.

I promised Sebastian, as he was placed in my arms for the first time, that I would give him all the happiness and all the love that the world had to offer.

As I look into his face now, his features sharp and distinctly Archibald, my heart tears in two.

I lift my hand, my fingers sprawling against his cheek.

"Does she love you?" I ask, already knowing the answer. He nods. "Then, we will find a way."

"You heard father. There is only one thing left to do and I'm not a fool. It won't go my way."

"Your father is cautious," I explain. "He knows that we are one of very few families that live truly happy lives in this town and he is cautious to bring unwanted attention upon us. Like from Lord Sinclair. He wants you to be happy too—"

"I will never be happy without her."

It was as if I have been thrown back in time and it is a young Harold Archibald, not Bash, standing in front of me, telling me with the deepest amount of certainty that when you know you know.

"I will help you." I curl my fingers under his chin, pulling his gaze to meet mine. "I will help you, and you and Tilly will be happy."

"How?" There is a scratch to his voice, like someone has torn through his lungs when they aimed for his heart and now he struggles to breathe.

I will do and give anything to fix it.

"Never mind. You leave it to me." I straighten his waistcoat. "Go and clean yourself up. We are expected to be at the Vances' in an hour."

I watch him ascend the staircase, disappearing as he rounds the corner at the top. I wring my fingers together in front of myself, thinking.

Catherine won't have lied to me, not after our honest conversation a few days ago. Not when she so desperately admitted that she wanted something different for Tilly.

I am an excellent judge of character, and after raising boys like Sebastian—as well as Freddy and Cassius, even if I only ever take credit for their decent manners and well-educated social sensitivities privately—I am no fool.

I know when I am being lied to.

No, Catherine seems to have no idea what is really going on.

I descend the narrow staircase hidden behind one of the fake paintings in the entrance hall, nodding politely to the cooks who are having their afternoon tea as I pass them on my way to the small study of my trusted housekeeper.

"Michaels?" The elderly woman stands from her desk even as I wave for her to not bother.

"My lady? What—Did you call for me? I did not hear the bell—"

"No no, I didn't call. I wanted to know whether ..." I take a deep breath.

Going through with this will mean doing the exact opposite to what Harold has asked of me and going against his words in pretty much every way.

But, then again, I wouldn't be the one physically getting in the way, so ...

"I wanted to know whether Nora had returned from her holiday visiting her Godmother in France."

"Nora? The housemaid from Winscombe House, my lady?"

"Yes, that Nora."

"I— Yes, I believe she returned last week."

I nod, the plot forming in my head quite clearly.

"Will you send for her? But, discreetly. Put her up in one of the nicer Inn's, one just outside of London. Somewhere safe and comfortable. I need to ask something of her and if it is to work, no one can know of her employment with us."

Michaels eyes me curiously and for a moment I think she may ask for more details. The questions obviously die on her tongue as the housekeeper simply nods and says, "Yes. Of course."

"Good." I turn for the door. "Oh—I would also appreciate it if you kept it quiet from the rest of the household. Especially ... Lord Archibald, yes?"

"Of course, my lady."

"Thank you, Michaels."

CHAPTER EIGHT

TILLY

The Vance family aren't as wealthy as some in town.

The Archibalds for one. Not even close to the Marsh's. And if Cassius cared enough about his own social standing, and stopped changing his mind about where he wanted to invest the family money he inherited, he'd probably be richer than the royal family themselves.

I am almost sure that he is some kind of cousin to the Queen. Of course, he refuses to confirm the rumour whenever I ask.

Still. The Vance's picnic was the event of the season. Year after year, it was one of the best on the calendar.

When I was little, it had been a family affair with children running eagerly from their tired nannies while lords and ladies sat idly by the water with glasses of chilled lemonade in hand.

There had been one year where Cassius had attended, a rare summer occasion where his parents had allowed him to come with them to London for the season. He'd been so shy that it had taken the coaxing of both Vivienne and I to get him to play with us. Freddy was staying with Bash's family, his father away again, and the five of us ran the entire circumference of the large pond that made up the gardens of the Vance's Estates.

Twice.

We've been inseparable since.

It is different now, though.

The five of us have grown up and at the same time so have the Vance sisters.

The picnic went from bare feet skipping through grass under the English summer sun to tightening a corset around my body sometime in the late afternoon and being pulled around a dance floor by twilight.

I attended the Vance evening picnic a few times already, prior to my own season, when Florence had waltzed with every available bachelor she could get her hands on. It's been years since then. It was a much simpler time when Bash swiped a bottle of chilled wine and led the five of us into the protection of the small woods nearby to drink and laugh.

Now I am tied into a dress that feels tight everywhere it shouldn't and my eyes itch. The heels on my feet hurt more than usual, my hair pins are too tight in places and too loose in others and all the while I have to bury my hands into the folds of my dress in order to hide the shaking.

I remind myself to keep a smile on my face, even if it hurts to do so.

Perhaps in another life, I may have been more open to the idea of marrying Elliot Sinclair.

Perhaps I may even like it.

There is no doubt that my father has arranged a solid engagement. Elliot is wealthy, already very popular in business, and he is set to inherit a high ranking title.

If anything, he could give me a very comfortable and easy life. There is a very good chance that he will be able to give me the two or three children I think I might like to have— a boy and a girl, at least.

It is easy to see that I could be running a sophisticated household that will keep me busy all year round, and I know that if I were to live in London full time there is a cause or two I think I might like to dedicate my brain power to.

In another life, I would probably think that he dances well with his tall frame that pulls me around the other couples easily. I may even like the way he wears his hair, short and neat with no strand out of place.

Perhaps if I was more like Florence I wouldn't have minded that he barely looks at me or that when he does, maybe as he directs a question or a comment at me, it is obvious that he stares at my shoulder instead of meeting my eyes.

In another life, maybe I wouldn't care all that much about being told who or when to marry.

But this isn't another life.

I stand idly by as my father speaks to Lord Sinclair. His tense shoulders and forced polite smile is mirrored in each and every one of us standing under lit lanterns and intricately designed canopies. Elliot Sinclair looks bored while his mother sips eagerly from the glass in her hand.

I cannot help turning away, allowing my mind to stray from the conversation and to search the crowd for the messy black hair and the easy grin.

Just a glance will settle my nerves and calm my racing pulse.

I stand between my own parents, eyes straying from the conversation and over the other guests.

In this life, I am in love with a man. He is not the one standing across from me as our parents discuss wedding details. He is not the much too polished gentleman that keeps casting a brunette across the room sideways glances.

I am in love with the messy and the carefree and the laughter.

I am in love with Sebastian Archibald, and no one will do but him.

I do not care for living in London full time, or for being another married Lady that has to spend her life turning the other way. I do not care for the picture of children with neat and tidy hair. I do not care for the life I am being sold into.

My parents are laughing so I laugh too. My parents smile so I smile too.

But I am lost.

I feel empty. Nothing that is said in the group—whether it is about business, or the wedding, or the weather—is heard when the hairs on the back of my neck stand up and I feel the pull of my stomach, the warmth spreading through me, starting from the spot on my neck I know he gazes at.

I lift a hand to the spot and stretch, trying to seem as natural as possible as I turn my head and search once more. It is inevitable, the heat I know is coming flares through my veins the moment I find him.

There.

His hazel eyes are bloodshot. His hair is a black mess of curls. His waistcoat is sitting a little contorted on his body and the jacket he has thrown over it is wrinkled. The fingers that hold a glass are raw and red and bruising.

He doesn't look away and neither do I.

"Matilda?" My mother's voice sounds muffled, as if it is the first sound I am hearing after an explosion.

"What?" I rip my eyes away from Bash. "I mean ... Sorry, pardon, I missed what you said?"

"Lady Sinclair is just asking if you had thought about what colour flowers you might like? For the wedding ..." My mothers brow furrows and the look of concern is written all over her face.

"I ... I don't ... No. I haven't thought about it." I tell them, my eyes stinging. "Will you excuse me? I'm feeling a little weary."

"Oh, did you want to sit down?" Lady Sinclair asks and I don't miss the small slur that catches her 's'. I watch the older woman bring the glass she holds to her lips, again, eyes closing as the remaining liquid drains in one go.

"I think I will take a walk. I think I may just need a little—" I look around as the noise of the conversations wash over me. It makes me sway where I stand. "Quiet."

My mother nods, as does Lady Sinclair, and before my father realises that I have excused myself, I head towards the pond.

There's a small embankment I know of just far enough from the party that I'll be able to lift the hem of my skirt and slip off my shoes. The water will be cool enough to rid my body of this uncomfortable heat that has been rising under my skin since I felt Bash's eyes on me.

The chatter subsides. The stifling over-scented air thins out. The further I walk, the more my muscles relax. It isn't until the candles lighting the party and its immediate surroundings dull that I realise he is behind me.

"Stop following me. You're only going to make this harder."

"No."

Despite everything, I laugh. But, as I do, the empty feeling in my chest pulses. The cracks of my heart ache with every breath.

I stand still, turning my face toward the water and fold my hands between the fabric of my dress. As my eyes close, I feel him moving around me. Hear the scuffle of shoes against stone pavements. Smell the indistinguishable scent of whiskey that pours from him as he snakes his arms around my waist.

"You shouldn't," I whisper. My body gives me away, as it always has when it comes to Bash. The moment his arms tighten around me I lean back into him. I roll my head back against his shoulder. His lips drop to my neck.

The sigh that leaves my lips is quiet and content.

Maybe I should have stayed at the party like a dutiful daughter.

Maybe I should be more like Florence and just marry who I'm told.

Maybe I should just smile at Elliot Sinclair, and laugh at his terrible jokes, and learn to turn away when he wanders off with another woman because that's what perfect, dutiful wives do.

But I can't. Bash exists and because he exists, I love him.

It is not possible to know him and not love him.

Not for me.

"I need to get back from the party," I say but I don't move.

"Not yet."

"My mother will be wondering where I am."

"Please. Stay," Bash says.

His hands drag gently across my stomach, fingers drifting over the delicate pearls that are sewn into the details of my corset. It's as if he is carving out pieces of my body. I am content to allow him.

No permission needed.

I stay silent, memorising the feel of his hands on me, as the dull music only just reaches where we stand. He lightly starts to sway. His face is still buried in my neck. His fingers still detail every inch of me.

I cling to them, a lifeline to the beating heart that I now share with him.

I want the moment to last forever. I want someone to paint us into a portrait that will hang on the walls of galleries, to immortalise us as one before the duties and the family-bound loyalties tear me from him forever.

"You're crying." A thumb reaches across my cheek delicately.

My breath shakes. "I am. I'm sad."

"Tils." His arms tighten and the cracks deepen. "It does not have to be this way."

I swallow, another tear falling freely and my eyes close before I push away from him.

His arms graze my waist, falling limply by his side as I move further out of his reach. "I can not have this conversation again. It is done, Bash. It's over."

"No."

"It is not that simple." All quiet contentment gone, my voice now drips with anger.

Anger that he does not understand, that he can not see from where he is standing in it all because, of course I want him. Of course, if I had a choice, there would be no question of it, no hesitation, none at all.

I move out of his grasp again as he reaches for me.

"It is simple, Tilly. You can make it simple," he pleads with me.

"What do you want from me, Bash?" His fingers enclose around my upper arm, sinking into the soft fabric as he squeezes, finally successful in closing the space between us.

But, even as he drags me back and everything about him overwhelms me, my throat still clenches as I fight to suppress more shuddering sobs. The scene begins to mirror the one only hours ago when we argued the same point.

"I do not have a choice."

Everything in his expression pleads with me. "Everyone has a choice."

"I do not."

"Yes, you do." For a moment, I glimpse the same burning anger twisting in amongst the soft gold and hazel of his eyes that had appeared back in my bedroom.

After a few beats Bash calms himself. His fingers loosen and he drops his forehead to mine, breathing me in.

"This cannot be how this goes. We all have a choice, just be brave enough to make it, even when we know our lives could be different because of it. We still have a—"

"Not me. Not about this. Not in my parents' eyes, not in society," I say.

I wish I could make him understand.

It is not the same for me. He would be forgiven. He would be welcomed back at his club with open arms and congratulatory handshakes. I would be whispered about. I would be shunned. My family would be shunned. My parents aren't perfect but I love them. A decision to run away with Bash would ruin them just as much as it would ruin me.

Society would turn their backs on us.

The thick evening air descends between Bash and I again, propelling me from him. He pauses for a moment and I allow myself to gulp air into my lungs. I wrap my arms around my middle and back into the protection of the small wood lining the pond.

Naturally, he follows. "I can't just let you go, Tilly. I can't sit back and watch you marry him, not when I lo—"

"Please do not." I round on him, a hand pressing into his chest and stopping his advance. "Please, do not say it."

"Fight for this, for us. Fight for me." He is broken, just as I am.

But unlike me, he is not quite defeated.

Instead, he is asking me to fight for him.

Standing in a place we once laughed as children, I rest so easily against his strong form and our future becomes clearer than the cloudless heavens above us. In the fading light of the moon, the gold flakes flash, dimming as my silence stretches on and I see him.

It is in the way he searches my face. In the heaving of his chest. In the thud of the heart that beats beneath my hand.

He doesn't think, doesn't believe that I will. The hand on his chest tightens, fingers clutching the fabric of his shirt, anchoring myself to him.

Fight for me.

It seemed so complicated, so out of my reach, as I read the letters on my father's desk. For years, I sat across from Florence and watched her be the perfect, dutiful daughter. I watched my older sister marry and fall pregnant within months. I watched how happy our parents were to announce their first grandchild. I listened to my mother gossip about newly announced engagements, never hesitating to pass judgement on the new couple's potential influence in society. I listened to her judge those who chose above or, God forbid, below their own station. I received scoldings when expressing the opinion that perhaps in some cases, love might be the principal reason for their pairing.

Eventually getting tired of arguments falling on deaf ears, I started to believe my mother; who promised me that love had no place in a marriage. Not at the beginning.

I was a rebellious child.

I climbed trees, and jumped into water, and held sticks up as if they were swords as I pretended to be a pirate. I scraped my knees and then kept running. I practiced the bow and arrow before the piano and I skipped my lessons, more than once, to learn how to ride a horse bareback, even after my father had strictly forbidden it.

Yet somewhere along the way and as I'd grown, my fingers began gliding across piano keys and the skirts I wore became far too heavy for running or climbing or jumping.

I forgot how to fight.

I wrench Bash toward me, meeting him messily in the middle as we come together.

He takes my face between his hands and kisses me.

Under his touch my head clears, the parchment on my father's desk is forgotten, the fallen tears rectified. The cracks in my heart begin to stitch themselves back together, one by one, as he tilts my face upward. A hand drops to my waist, squeezing, before wrapping around me and pulling me in tighter.

I curl my arms around his neck, fingers digging into his hair. When he moves, I move with him. My back hits the trunk of a tree, his hand protecting against the impact.

As his lips move down my neck, I inhale the light, summer air desperate to refill my lungs. A small whimper drops from my lips as he sweeps across my collarbone, sucking at the exposed skin. My breasts swell as he drags his mouth lower, teeth grazing the top of my corset.

"Are you ... I'm sorry. I shouldn't have—" Bash pulls away from me.

"Shut up." I laugh. My body shivers at the loss of his warmth so I tug him back to me. This time, he is slower with his exploration of my mouth.

He swipes his tongue across mine before I feel his teeth lightly pull at my bottom lip, making me arch into him as something white hot and erotic twists within me.

With a groan, he tears himself from me and rests his forehead on mine. His attention still on my heaving chest, I curl his messy hair around my fingers. "My eyes are up here, Archibald."

A smirk settles across his mouth like an old friend. "Sorry."

"You are forgiven." I smile, reaching up to press another kiss against the corner of his mouth. I can feel something pressing into my hip and when I move, just a little, he grabs my waist to stop me.

"Stop moving like ... just ... stay there." There is a husk to his voice that I don't recognise, one that I haven't heard before. Something floods through me, making me shiver and my thighs press together.

"What is it? Did I do something wrong?" This draws a short burst of laughter from him and it cuts through the quiet that surrounds us like a knife.

"No, no. Never."

"Then what—" I reach down, my hand brushing against him. "Oh."

His laugh this time is strained but softer, the redness creeping across his face, the embarrassment obvious amongst his tight features. "You ... should go. I will ... I will follow you, in a moment."

"I do not want to go." I tuck my fingers behind his neck, holding him to me, as if I want to lock myself in place.

Another groan. This time, it's my name. "Prescott."

"Archibald," I mimic his tone, teasing. He bends to kiss me again and I let him.

"I want to fight for this. For you," I murmur when we break apart. His shoulders relax under my touch and his chest releases with a relieved exhale.

"Then we fight," he says.

Any words of reply are swallowed as he presses himself against me again. The kiss is heated with such intensity that my stomach clenches and my legs shake a little as I cling to him.

I need more.

More of him, more of this.

Much more.

Instinctively, I roll my hips into his and he pulls back, hissing again.

"What?" I demand. "Tell me what that means."

I slide a hand down his chest, my fingers feeling the way his muscles flex beneath them even through the layers he wears.

"God, I forgot that mothers teach their daughters nothing about anything."

"What has this got to do with my mother?" I ask, brows furrowing. It makes Bash laugh, shaking his head.

"Nothing." He takes the hand I slid down his chest and places it over his heart which beats heavily beneath it. "You do this to me. You, and you alone, do this."

"I don't understand."

"What do you feel, right now, between your ..." He stutters, words failing him as I watch expectantly. "What do you feel?"

I swallows, "I—"

It's not as if I cannot find the words to explain it. More like, I can, but they are possibly the most indecent thoughts I've ever had.

"It's like there's a knot in my stomach. But it's not really in my stomach, it's ... lower." I lick my bottom lip, pulling it between my teeth.

"Do you ... have you ever ... tried to untie it?" he asks. I shake my head as he folds his fingers into the skirt of my dress, clenching the fabric into his fist.

"Can you?" I ask. His face flames, the deepest of reds spreading up his neck as he drops his head to my shoulder. A groan pulls deep from his chest.

"You do not have to. I just thought … how do I learn?" I say quickly, worried that I've gone too far.

"Learn?" He asks, still buried into my shoulder.

"Well, yes. You said mothers do not teach their daughters anything, and you obviously know about it so I'm assuming others do too. Does Cassius? Vivi?"

I feel his smile in the kiss he presses to my neck. "I would almost guarantee that they do."

"I want to learn." I say, more confidently.

"Only you, Matilda Prescott, would turn this moment into something educational." He pulls back from me. "Are you sure?"

"Yes." I am breathless under his heated gaze.

"This is not something everyone just … does." He slowly gathers my dress in his hand, catching the hem as his fingers graze against my stockings. My breathing hitches as he says, "We cannot take this back. You have to be sure."

Our gaze meets and I know that what we are about to do will entwine us inextricably for the rest of our lives.

With most of high society only a hundred or so meters away, with Bash smelling like whiskey and fire wood, with my dress bunching around my waist and his fingers dragging along the soft skin of my thigh, I tilt my head up to meet his lips.

"I want all of my firsts to be with you. Only with you."

In another life, I may have stayed by my mother's side at the party. In another life, I may make a different choice. But this wasn't another life and even if it was, I don't think my pathway would've been any different.

He kisses me, pressing me against a tree in the wood we played in as children. His fingers caress the inside of my thigh, dragging along my soft skin and permanently marking me.

Falling in love with Sebastian Archibald was unavoidable. In this life or any other I might have lived, because under his touch, I feel safe. Under his touch, I let go.

Under his touch, I breathe a symphony of sighs.

His fingers brush the heat between my legs causing me to jolt forward and bury my face into his shoulder. He slowly draws patterns on my skin. Heat coils in my stomach, an ache starting deep within me and growing as he continues.

"Bash," I breathe, his name falling from my lips in a pitch I'd never known myself to make.

"Does it feel good?" He murmurs, continuing his patterns. My thighs are becoming sticky and wet and hot. The ache is spreading. I'm clutching Bash with all of my strength.

It feels so good.

I can't talk, I can't think. I look up, finding his eyes on me and I nod. He draws the wetness downward and slips a single finger inside my body. I whimper, lifting enough on my toes to kiss him again. With the strokes of his thumb and the curl of his fingers, I cling to his body as a fire rages through me.

My knee hitches at his hip, foot curling around his leg for stability as his finger dives into me, over and over again.

My head rolls back and I begin to see stars behind my closed lids.

I know he is watching me. I know, just like me, he is probably working to ingrain this moment in his memory. When I feel the pull to meet his gaze, the intense hazel burns into my soul. He sees right to my core and he leaves his name carved in my heart.

So I do the same.

The flames race through my veins. His pace picks up. My head tilts and my mouth falls open in a silent scream of pleasure as Bash murmurs words I never want to forget. "Let go, Tils. I've got you."

And he does.

As he eases my feet back to the ground, the pulsing between my legs fading, his hand reappears from beneath my skirt, glistening. I can't help but watch, captivated, as he pulls a handkerchief from his pocket and wipes them clean.

He replaces the square piece of cloth into his pocket, his other hand still at my waist. He stands unbelievably close to me, not allowing much to come between us. But I find that there is nothing to complain about. I still shake and I am sure that I am not quite ready for him to be out my reach, not yet.

"I want to fight." I whisper, resting my head against his shoulder.

He jostles. "Huh?"

"I want to fight, and—" I lift my head. "I love you, too."

"Then, we fight."

And with those words, the mark he left on my soul burns.

As I look at Bash, the moonlight peaking through the trees that shield us from above and the thought of leaving this secluded corner enters my mind, my heart aches.

There is no staying away from him.

I know now that not a time will come that I won't feel his touch on my body, pressing hotly into my skin or wrapping tightly around my waist to keep me steady.

Not a time that I won't think of all the ways he said my name: in laughter, in frustration, in happiness, in desire.

I will remember that the most.

We are tangled together in every way I'd ever want and yet, not in the way that truly matters.

"Will you stay with me tonight? After the party, will you sneak in however you sneak in and stay with me?"

He only kisses me in reply and that is enough.

For now.

CHAPTER NINE
BASH

Time makes a mockery of us.

I stay. Because how could I not?

I am a mere mortal man and she is a siren calling my name in one of the many whispered signs she's carved into my skin.

We spend each day together, chaperoned and in the company of our friends. Each evening, in ballgowns and dress tails, she asks me to stay. Each night, I sneak in.

It seems that there is more to learn, to touch, to soak in of Matilda Presott than time is allowing.

The way she looked at me that first night, the one after I took her against a tree, when she opened her door to me, is etched into my brain. Her hair fell over her shoulders in loose curls and her smile brightened my entire world. She wore the same cream gown that I bunched around her waist in the woods yet she'd taken her shoes off.

I made a joke about her height and she'd swatted at my arm. I caught her wrist and dragged her into me. I remember how she watched my hand lift slowly, my thumb freeing her lip and running over soft skin, her eyes flashing before she tilted her face to mine.

We took our time—not knowing, not understanding, just how little we truly had yet— finding a pace somewhere between the soft, slow movement of our first kiss and the heated, passionate, insatiable mess that was our coming together in the woods.

She didn't move to revisit our actions in the woods, nor had I pushed it. The first night I spent with Matilda was spent whispering stories and secrets on her bedroom floor. We fell asleep facing one another, arms outstretched, fingers reaching for one another.

So, even as Freddy thoroughly warns against it—even as Cassius thoroughly encourages it—I continue to return to her side, after twilight subsides and the society of London returns to their summer houses.

As another night falls like a well-kept promise at the end of each day, I sneak through the corridors of her childhood home. Under the same roof that her parents sleep soundly, I close the door to her bedroom and lock us inside. With the click of the lock, we take time back into our own hands.

Quiet confessions pass, unspoken between us, as my hazel falls deep into her emerald when she looks at me. I greet her with a soft kiss and she melts into me.

Tilly falls asleep in the early hours of the morning, after we both go quiet and I am content to listen to her breathing deepen while tracing the edges of her fingers, her hands, her body. I commit it all to memory.

Our future is entirely uncertain.

When the sun still follows nightfall hours later it feels more and more like a betrayal with each passing day. Time laughs, openly and loudly, as we walk the fine line between freely falling in love and protecting ourselves from the inevitable heartbreak that solidifies itself with every traitorous sunrise.

But when she faces me in her sleep with her hair splayed across a pillow and her robe loosened as her chest rises and falls, I take the opportunity in the quiet moments of the morning to brush stray hair from her face.

To watch the way her eyes flutter beneath her closed lids.

"I can feel you staring at me. Stop it," she whispers.

I smile. "No."

"It is odd."

"I like the view."

She sighs with a small tug of a smile evident on her lips, her leg shifting over mine as she pulls herself closer to curl against me. She rests her head on my shoulder, her nose buries into the cotton of my shirt. I slip an arm around her waist, securing her in place, and tuck my chin to kiss her hair.

"What time is it?" She asks.

I eye the clock above her mantel, heart jumping at the late morning hour. I know that once I tell her, Tilly will scramble from my arms at the indecency of it all. I linger a little when I drop my lips back to her hair.

"Just after nine," I murmur.

As expected, Tilly jolts out of my arms and stumbles across the room. She shakes the door handle to confirm that it is still locked from the night before.

"God, Bash," she breathes out. I laugh, pushing up on my elbows to watch as she leans against the door in relief. "Stop laughing, if we had been caught—"

"But we were not." I hold a hand out, asking for her to join me back in bed and revel in the silence of our morning for just a moment longer.

"It is careless—"

The sharp knock on her bedroom door cuts through her reply.

The hourglass that we are fighting effortlessly tips and the sand races through. My tentative hold on another quiet morning breaks and the moment is gone.

Her eyes widen as I sit up, shaking my head. My eyes darted around the room, trying to find a place to hide.

"Matilda? Darling, It is already nine o'clock. You promised to go with Vivienne to Agatha's for tea this morning. She will be here soon." Catherine Prescott is not a frightening woman. In fact I like her quite a lot, having been on the receiving end of her kind hugs and encouraging smiles since I was a child. But I doubt they would continue if she found me sprawling across her daughter's bed.

Clothed or not.

"I am awake. One moment." The door handle rattles, still firmly locked. Tilly turns her eyes back on me, whispering, "Under the bed. Now."

"What?"

"Get under the bed, Archibald, now." I obey, the stern cut of her words reminding me absurdly of my own mother. "And hush"

As I curl beneath her bed, the dust ruffle falling into place to cover me in darkness, I dare to imagine the look on Freddy's face when I eventually tell him about this. I know, without any doubt, that Cassius will never let me live this down and—if by some miracle I'm the one Tilly meets at the end of the aisle—I know that Cassius will be retelling it to every child, every grand-child, that might ever come from us.

"Sorry, Mother, I must've—" There's hesitation in Tilly's tone and it makes my fingers twitch. "I hadn't meant to lock it."

There is a beat of silence.

"It's quite alright darling. I wanted to speak with you for a moment anyway."

"Oh?"

"Your father wants to tell you, but he has been rather insen-sitive lately and I'm afraid he doesn't quite understand."

"What is it, Mother?"

I can only imagine the frown that falls on Catherine's face at the impatience in Tilly's tone.

"Your father and Lord Sinclair requested the marriage license yesterday afternoon. They expect it to all go through ... and you will be married at the end of the month."

"This month?"

"I ... Yes."

"Three weeks away?"

"If it all goes to their plan, yes, but Tilly—"

"You can leave, now." I flinch. Tilly's words are harsh, cracked and barely audible, but even from my position under the bed, I can tell her face is likely set, holding a masked expression of indifference.

"Tilly, please." A scuffle of footsteps and a squeak of bed-springs. The mattress above me dips. Catherine is sitting on the edge of the bed. "I know that I have always said love had no place and I know that Florence was perfectly happy to—"

"You let it happen." Again my fingers twitch, wanting nothing more than to reach for Tilly. To hold her in my arms and make the sadness, the disappointment in her tone, disappear. "You let this happen. You are my mother, you are supposed to know, to see ..."

"I know. I know and I'm so sorry, Matilda—"

The springs squeak again as Catherine's weight lifts off the bed.

There is silence before I hear Tilly's muffled tone. "I need to get ready for tea at Agatha's."

"Matilda ..." Catherine sighs, but then her footsteps retreat. "Alright."

I wait for the footsteps to disappear, for the door to click shut, and for the lock to turn.

I wait for it to be clear to move and not a moment longer.

Rolling out from under the bed, I push up on my knees and immediately search for Tilly. She sits on the carpeted floor, knees tucked into her chest with her arms around herself. Her head rests on her knees. Her body jerks forward, just slightly. It's her only tell that she is struggling to hold herself together.

I cross the room, dropping back to my knees in front of her. "Tils?"

A fresh crack appears in my heart as she lifts her head, eyes red, to meet my gaze.

"She is supposed to know, even if he does not. She is my mother ..." Tilly whispers.

"I know." I sit back, reaching for her to follow me. Her knees fall on either side of me, her head falling to my shoulder, and her arms tightening around my neck as she silently asks me to keep her together.

As she can no longer.

I am right then.

Time does make a mockery of us.

It laughs at our misfortune. At our heartbreak.

As we scramble to slow the expeditiously falling sand, to shatter the hourglass altogether, it sits and watches and laughs.

Perhaps before an end date had been set, I could've convinced myself that I may have found a way. A solution. Maybe, before the papers had been drawn and the licenses requested, I might have laughed at the prospect of Tilly ending up with someone else.

Three weeks.

Twenty one days.

Twenty one nights.

Then she becomes someone else's.

In some cruel twist, some terrible event, some misstep of fate, I am going to lose her and there doesn't seem to be anything I can do to stop it.

CHAPTER TEN
TILLY

"WHY ARE YOU WEARING black?" Vivi asks, eyeing me closely.

Lifting a glass of champagne to my lips, I find where my father stands. He watches me from the other side of the ballroom with a distasteful expression.

"Because I am in mourning."

My friends and I stand behind a few opulently decorated tables filled with food and refreshments. Fabric hangs from the ceiling to create the silhouette of a canopy and lit candles cover the walls. People are everywhere and the room is stifling with the heavy scent of mismatched perfumes.

My senses are overwhelmed but a laugh–*his* laugh–cuts through the noise and warms me. A hand traces down my spine and leaves me shivering in its wake. Everything dulls; the noise, the scent, the lighting. Bash comes into focus and takes over.

"Who died?" Bash asks. Even though I know it's a bad idea, I lean back into his chest. He takes my weight and I look up at him, smiling. I glance around the room and catch my father's gaze again.

"My freedom," I say, not breaking eye contact.

"And you call me dramatic," he whispers in my ear. Another shiver rolls down my back.

Freddy groans as he takes a step sideways to hide the fact that Bash has curled his fingers around my hip and pulled me further into him.

"Could you two please remember that we are in public," he says, exasperated.

"So?" I smirk over my glass before lifting it to my lips only to have Bash steal it from my hand. "Excuse me."

"You are excused." He downs the rest of the liquid, throwing his head back.

I focus on how the muscles in his neck tense. On how easily the liquid slides down. The way his Adam's apple bobs as his throat tightens. The movement sends an electric current shooting through my nerves. I remember the way they moved under my lips. The way he felt when I kissed him. I spent hours over the last week learning him as if I was drawing a detailed map of his body.

Bash catches my gaze and the hand resting on my hip squeezes. The hazel pools of his eyes swirl and darken, just as they do right before he drops his mouth to mine and I lose myself in the feeling of his hands on my body.

"God. Cassius and Vivienne are more discreet than the two of you. Do I have to remind you that Tilly is engaged—"

"No, Freddy, you do not," I interrupt, annoyance cutting into my words. Bash spreads his fingers against my hip, pulling me closer to him. I look up at him again. "A dance, Bash? Please?"

"As you wish." He places the now empty glass on a table nearby before he holds out his free hand.

I slide my palm into his. Our hands fit together perfectly and I pull him toward the middle of the crowded room. His fingers glide effortlessly over the small of my back as he draws me closer to him. I slip my hand behind his neck, fingers pausing momentarily when they instinctively curl into his hair before I slide them further down his shoulder to rest at a more appropriate place. I look up into his face and the room fades away.

Amongst the twirling skirts and flickering coat tails, Bash leads me around the dance floor. He drops his head close to mine, his mouth on my ear.

"Freddy means well," he says. Safe in his arms, my eyes close. Bash continues to guide me around the room with all the other people. The insistent mothers and bored fathers and eligible suitors are distant blurs. "He is concerned for your reputation more than anything. But also the consequences if we are caught. He knows it isn't how you want this to happen."

I sigh, my hand tightening in his. "We just won't get caught, then."

"Huh." His quiet chuckle sends warmth running through my veins. "And how many times have you snuck out of your bedroom before sunrise this week?"

"None." I turn my head, my smile hidden as I press my face as deep into his shoulder as I dare.

"And how many times have you hid under a bed to avoid getting caught?"

"None."

"Exactly."

He smirks. Amusement is front and centre in his eyes and they sparkle, but it's dimmed. I can still see the endless pit of fears that lie beneath.

The distress. The worry. The complete uncertainty.

I stop myself from leaning up on my toes and kissing him. Under all my own jokes, all my own smiles, under the amour of simply pretending my impending marriage doesn't exist, I feel all the same emotions as Bash.

Distress. Worry. Complete uncertainty.

My eyes flicker to his lips.

"I love you," I murmur. "You know that, right?"

Bash nods, the hazel in his eyes darkening once more as his hand slips lower on my back.

Eleanor

"They are being a little obvious, are they not?" Catherine whispers to me with her lips hidden behind her champagne glass as we watch our children waltz amongst the rest of the guests.

I watch as Bash laughs and then drops his head, whispering something that makes Tilly's lips turn up in a smile in return. They seem to move as one, fitting easily against one another as if they have been cut from the same tree only to be shaped and polished over the years before meeting again to still find they are each one half of a whole.

While I know it is unwise and I know that the inevitable conversation I will have to have with my son will fall on deaf ears, I can't help but allow my heart to grow warm in the glow that radiates from the two of them.

They are perfect together.

"I will speak with Bash later," I reply. It's the only thing I can say even though I doubt very much it will do any good.

"Forbidding them will simply propel them further," Catherine says in agreement, scoffing a little behind her glass.

"I agree," I tilt my head a little closer to Catherine's, my voice lowering to almost a whisper. "Is he still sneaking into the house each night?"

"Yes. I think it is absolutely adorable that they think they could do so without notice." She shakes her head.

The night after the Vance's picnic, I watched my son cross the cobble-paved street from my bedroom window. He shoved his hand deep in his pockets and his eyes roamed the empty street. I woke during the night and as I made my way toward the staircase for the kitchen, I pushed open the door to Bash's room only to find it empty, the sheets folded down on his bed by the housekeeper and untouched.

"I remember what it was to be young and madly in love." My eyes drift across the room in search of my husband. Harold speaks with Cassius and Vivienne, smiling easily at the pair as they chat. Harold is an old friend of Vivienne's father and we have had the pleasure of watching her grow up.

Cassius seems focused on Vivienne's face and when she smiles, his expression relaxes easily. I smile. That boy can fight it as long as he pleases but I know that in the end he will be asking for the youngest Pembroke daughter's hand. It may take another year or two, stubborn as Cassius is in his view about marriage.

But they will get there.

Just as I hope Bash and Tilly will.

"Tilly is bolder than I was. Than Jonathan ever was," Catherine murmurs quietly next to me.

As if she summoned him, Jonathan appears at Catherine's side. I don't miss the tight grip of his fingers on my friend's elbow or the grimace that crosses Catherine's face before she tugs her arm free.

"Go and tell your daughter she is to dance with Elliot Sinclair," Jonathan says into Catherine's ear. He very much should work on his volume control. His words are crisp and clear although I am sure his words were not intended for me. I frown but turn away anyway, giving the appearance of privacy.

"She is embarrassing the family hanging off Archibald's arm like that," Jonathan continues.

"Jonathan—" Catherine begins.

My eyes dart about the room, finding the haunting figure of Lord Sinclair who happens to be watching my son and Tilly with an expression that sends chills down my spine.

He is dangerous.

Harold has started to remind me of this at every opportune moment. It is not something I have considered much. But right now–staring at the young couple in the middle of the dance floor–he looks dangerous.

The way Lord Sinclair eyes Bash makes my stomach twist and I suddenly feel the urge to unsheathe the ceremonial sword that sits at his side and run him through with it myself.

Unfortunately, polite society dictates I turn to alternative measures of sabotage.

Like Nora.

"No, Catherine. I have told you this many times." My attention pulls back to the couple at my side, Jonathan's voice dripping as if sour whiskey. I am sure he has probably drowned himself tonight. "I will not condone this. I am the head of this family. I make the decisions. You and Matilda will obey them."

I straighten my shoulders feeling the anger beginning to bubble in my veins. As if he can feel me from across the room, my eyes meet Harold's. He is clearly scrutinising the situation and trying to determine what might be happening now that Jonathan has joined Catherine and I.

His eyes roam over me, narrowing as he watches me lift my glass to my lips and raise my brows at him. His features harden and he shakes his head, as if to say, do not get involved.

Too late.

My mind wanders briefly to my secluded lunch with Nora a few days earlier, after the young girl arrived from Wescombe.

"I will not be a part of this any longer." Catherine's words twist into a harsh command. I have never heard such confidence from my friend. "Unlike you, I want Matilda to be happy. So if you want her to dance with Sinclair, or separate her from Sebastian, then you are more than welcome to go and tell her yourself. I will not play this game with you anymore."

"It does not matter. The marriage will go ahead." Something vicious drips from his tone and it causes my stomach to twist just as it had done when I saw the dark expression upon Lord Sinclair's face. It sets my nerves on edge. "The license has been granted. Lord Sinclair is agreeable and we have set the date for a week. It is done. What you think or what Matilda wants does not matter."

"How dare—"

I turn to the couple.

"Perhaps," I begin, my gaze falling on Jonathon's hard expression. I do not miss the way Catherine's glass shakes from the confrontation. "This may not be the time nor the place to have this discussion."

"Forgive me, Lady Archibald—" Again I find myself frowning. When did I become Lady Archibald to my friend? At least someone I considered a friend. "But you do not have the right to an opinion here. You have been filling my wife's head with nonsense for months. Nonsense that some type of deal had already been struck between us in regards to our children and their future."

"I would advise—" Harold's familiar touch sends shivers up my spine as his chest presses against my back. His hand grips my hip and pulls me to him. For a moment I remember watching Bash do the same only minutes before Tilly dragged him to the middle of the twirling dances, and I am struck— again— by just how similar my boys are. "— that you watch your tone when speaking to my wife."

"Archibald." Jonathan says as he stiffens.

"I believe the deal you are referring to is merely a conversation that has passed between our two families since Bash came home from school. I understand no formal agreement was struck, however I think we can all agree we thought it unnecessary considering how clearly in love our children are with each other."

There is no way to stop it so I don't bother to try.

Smugness radiates from me and a smirk settles across my lips. It washes over Jonathan in the form of a paling complexion, a narrowed eye, and a scoff before an abrupt exit from our conversation.

Around us the dancers still twirl and the ton still chatters.

"A week," Catherine whispers, voicing all our fears and throwing them into the open as if they are less terrifying that way.

I find our children still spinning amongst the crowd. Matilda's red hair rippling down her back as her head tilts upward to Sebastian's. Bash's lips move as he speaks quietly to her. But his eyes are trained closely on us as he watches the exchange with a hint of panic in his eyes.

I force a smile and ignore my own panic as it begins to grow in my chest.

"I was hoping we would have more time," I say. It earns me a worried look from Catherine and a gentle squeeze from Harold. "Nora may not find anything in a week. It could take a while for her to gain their trust."

"Nora? As in *our* Nora?" Harold handles me like a puppet, hand tugging at the right pieces of fabric to have me twist in his arms.

I ignore him. The carefully planned steps that I have already set in motion run through my mind over and over. We will need to move it along. To speed it up. Nora needs time she no longer has. It will have been for nothing if she finds nothing.

My instinct tells me she will, though, so I steal my nerves and take a steadying breath.

"Eleanor, what have you done?" Harold asks sternly.

"Nothing. Nothing." I reply, shouting a warning glance at Catherine so she doesn't speak.

Harold opens his mouth, likely wanting to press the issue because he definitely knows I am lying to him. Thankfully, a deep voice calls out for him and I am saved. He pierces me with one last stare before following the voice to a group of men near the drinks service.

"I will be answering to that later," I sigh.

"What are we to do?" Catherine whispers, turning toward me. "A week is hardly any time."

I set the glass I am still holding on a nearby table, take Catherine's hand in my own and pat it gently as my eyes find our children again. Bash and Tilly have rejoined the others and all five now stand in a shadowed corner of the room. Bash stands between Freddy and Cassius as they laugh about something. Closing off their circle, with their backs to Catherine and I, Tilly and Vivienne stand with their heads together, whispering.

"I have sent one of my housemaids to work for Sinclair."

"You—what?!" Catherine squeaks, stepping back in surprise and almost hitting one of the poor footmen carrying a tray with newly filled champagne flutes. I give him a tight smile before taking one from the tray.

"It is risky but something is telling me those Sinclairs are hiding something," I reply quietly.

I watch as Bash pulls Tilly toward him. The boys move around them, blocking them from view but not well enough. Bash shifts and bends down. I don't miss the gentle kiss he presses to Tilly's neck, nor do I miss the soft smile that spreads across the young girl's face when he does.

It's easy and quiet and so effortlessly natural.

They fit.

Perfectly together.

Made for one another.

Frustration fills me and anxiety twists within me as it mixes with my motherly instinct to ensure happiness at all costs. I am powerless here. I cannot control the results.

I do not like it. Not one bit.

"What do we do?" Catherine says, watching the couple as I do.

"Pray that Nora succeeds."

Chapter Eleven
Nora

I LEAN AGAINST THE wall, hiding in a small alcove as I catch my breath. This household has many problems, but the first is that the family seems to be allergic to opening a bloody window. The air is stuffy and carries the distinct smell of cigars.

Lord Sinclair smokes almost constantly. I am yet to see him without one hanging out of the side of his mouth. I crinkle my nose. I miss the country. I miss Wescombe house.

I flinch a little, my hand flying to my chest, when the door next to my hiding spot rattles. Someone slams the front door as they come through to the foyer of the house.

"I am bored of the game, father," the voice of Master Elliot Sinclair is muffled through the door. I glance down the narrow corridor for any other servants before stepping closer to the hidden door and pressing my ear against it. "She is not interested. Archibald will find a way to get in the way. He always does."

My heart skips a beat and I press myself closer to the door. This is it. They are talking about Master Archibald. This is why I am here.

"I have a contract," someone replies. I suck in a breath and hold it. It's Lord Sinclair. "It is happening."

"This was fun but now ..."

"Now, what?" Lord Sinclair asks. His voice is close. Very close. I close my eyes and imagine they stand just on the other side of the large family portrait that hides the door to the corridor leading to the servants quarters and kitchens. The same corridor I currently hide in.

"I do not know if I want to marry the Prescott girl." I note the slight whine in the younger Sinclair's voice. Like a toddler about to throw a tantrum. I roll my eyes. "She's a bore and I ... I have lost interest."

Lord Sinclair scoffs and lets out a sharp laugh.

"I know very well where your interest sits," he says. "And I am telling you right now, it will never happen. You need to stop chasing silly ideals and grow up. You are the future Lord Sinclair and you need to act like it."

"But ..."

"No buts. No more midnight strolls. No more late night visitors. They are done. *You* are done. Focus on the Prescott girl and the business she stands in the way of."

There's a pause. Silence falls and I press my ear hard to the door. Midnight strolls? Elliot is leaving the house at night? And getting visitors?

This conversation is just getting more and more confusing. But, at the very least, I can send word that my Lady was right.

Something is not right in this house and with this family

"Yes, father."

CHAPTER TWELVE
TILLY

I think of Bash the entire carriage ride home.

My mother is abnormally quiet so my thoughts are free to wander. I already miss him. I barely just left him and I am already eager to be back in his arms.

I am counting the minutes until he arrives at my bedroom door tonight.

We walk through the door to our London home, and without wishing my mother goodnight, I make my way to the stairs while bunching the black silk in my hand to prevent it from dragging along the floor.

My mourning dress.

I thought it was clever. Vivi laughed as she ran her fingers over the beading as we caught our breath between dances. She also told me that it was far too gorgeous for one to wear to a funeral.

She's right, so I promised her I never would.

Then Bash dragged me into the corner of the room and pressed his lips to my neck. Right there, in the open. Where anyone could've seen us. My heart raced with adrenaline.

"You would look far better in white. Don't you think?"

His whispered words had sent a warm shiver down my spine, heating my body and coiling the need for him within my stomach. I simply smiled and pushed my hips back into him, just a little. That earnt me a low, mumbled groan and another squeeze of his fingers against my waist.

"Matilda." My mother's voice pulls me from my thoughts. I pause on the stairs and ignore the ache of my feet. I turn to her, the black silk swishing as a sway on the steps.

"Yes?" I reply.

"I—" As my mother stutters, I feel the content pleasure that has been buzzing beneath my skin throughout the night and since leaving Bash's side begin to subside. Its absence paves the way for the droplets of doubt, of anxiety, of pure terror to infiltrate my veins. I watch my mother sigh and her eyes fill with tears.

"Your father has told me that the marriage license has been approved. Lord Sinclair has insisted on a date within the week. Your father has agreed."

For a moment I have been dreading, it seems odd that I am overwhelmed with the urge to laugh.

For a smile to break my hardened features and to laugh.

Because surely not.

Deep down, a small part of me believed my parents might have been playing some sort of cruel practical joke. It is a small part of me, but a part of me nonetheless.

Laughter bubbles in my chest, threatening to burst out as I stare at my mother.

A joke.

It is a joke that my mother is standing in front of me, close to tears, when it isn't *her* happiness on the line. It isn't the rest of *her* life that Father is throwing away. It isn't the love of *her* life that is being torn from her.

"You ... you cannot be serious," I say, fighting against the laughter as anger begins to burn through me. My mother nods and the action breaks my resolve.

I laugh.

Head shaking and fingers burning themselves in the fabric of my dress, I pick up my skirt, take two steps at a time down the stairs, and head for my father's office.

This time when I open the door the fire is roaring and it casts a bright glow about the room. The corners are brightened further with candles and my father sits with his head dipped to the side and his eyes half closed, twirling a feather quill in his hand.

I throw open the door, recklessly and with little care to its ageing hinges. My father titters as the heavy wooden door hits the wall with a thump.

"Careful, darling. You will wreck the wallpaper doing that. Your mother just redecorated."

"Why should I care?" I spit out, the laughter turning vile in my throat. "You will have no use for this house once you are dead. Florence has a London home already and you are signing my life away to a permanent prison. I shall be locked away in the Sinclair Residence for the rest of my days."

"Matilda—"

"Ah, or perhaps you care for the state of this house more than your own daughter's happiness?" My father opens his mouth but I cut off his reply with a vicious, burst of twisted laughter falling from my lips. "You must do it. You must because you have agreed to marry me off. You have sentenced me yourself."

"That is enough, Matilda. I will not tolerate this any longer." My father stands behind his desk, his hand clutching the edge to support his weight. I can tell this argument is weighing on his already poor health but I find I no longer care. At some point between coming so close to having the man I love and so far from actually being with him, Bash has become the only thing I truly care for anymore.

Him, and our friends.

"I cannot marry him." My chest restricts. My voice cracks. I feel my resolve going much the same way. Still standing at my side, my mother reaches for my hand and squeezes.

My shoulders square and I turn my gaze in time to see my mother jut out her chin, her watery expression now replaced with a much harder mask. She's switched sides and now we face a common enemy.

"Jonathan, you must see reason," Mother says.

"Catherine, enough. I have already said I will no longer tolerate this. It has been decided."

"But Sebastian—"

"No, Catherine. The Archibald boy does not change anything now." Father's hands shake as he pours scotch into a glass.

"Why?" I am seething, my skin feeling as if it is on fire. I am too hot in my dress, too angry at the tears that I know will burn once they fall. "Why doesn't he change things? I love him. You are sentencing me to a life of unhappiness if you do not allow me to be with him."

"It is bigger than you, Matilda. You know this. The ink is dry."

"So rip up the parchment!" My voice echoes off the wood panelled walls. My father cringes. "Please, please …" My voice cracks and I can no longer hold my tears at bay.

My cheeks are wet. As if they are acid, the tears burn themselves a path down my cheeks. Trailing the curves of my face, staining my skin on their way.

"I will do anything, *anything*. Please do not make me do this," I plead.

"Florence is perfectly happy with her arrange—"

"I am not Florence!"

It is childish, I know this, to stomp my foot and demand he hear me. But after all our differences growing up, how could my father truly compare my sister and I in something as fundamental as love?

Florence has never loved like I do. Florence has never had her own Bash. She was compliant and willing to go into her arrangement because she simply wanted to be married, to be a mother.

I want to marry *Bash*.

To be a mother to *Bash's* children.

The tears blur my vision for a moment. I blink them away and when they clear, my father's face comes into view. Jonathon Prescott looks resolute. Hardened. As if he is no longer willing to listen to reason. As if he is unable to see how my heart shatters into a million pieces of sharp glass at my feet due to this unwavering resolve.

"It would cost this family gravely to back out of such an agreement. The Sinclair's have bought into our business on one condition. That you and Elliot marry." My father sits back in his chair, resting his head in his hands. He is no longer able to look at me. "We would have to buy them out of the contract, out of the business. A clause I thought nothing of because how could I have known that you would fall in love with the Archibald boy?"

"Oh, Jonathan." My mother pulls me into her chest, wrapping my shaking body up in her arms. "How could you not?"

***

Earlier this evening when under the heavily perfumed atmosphere of yet another ball, in yet another ballroom, I joked with my friends that I am in mourning.

But now I feel as if I really am grieving.

No longer for my freedom. It is clear to me *that* is already lost.

But for a life.

A life that when I close my eyes and dream of Bash, seems bright and happy, effortless and comforting. Clear air of the countryside. Children's laughter carrying on the wind. Mornings of waking in his arms and nightfalls kissing him until my heart's content. A family. A husband. A life full of love and laughter and light.

All gone.

Bash slips into my room, the door opening with the slightest sound of ageing hinges. I don't bother to raise my head to look at him but keep my eyes unfocused and toward the ceiling.

The lock clicks and the bed dips.

"Tils?" His voice warms me, brings me joy and happiness at the same moment as it breaks my heart. Fingers search for my ankle beneath the ruffles of fabric that still surround me and my almost lifeless form. I didn't bother undressing.

One touch, as gentle as a calm breeze on a warm day, and his palm begins to warm my freezing form instantly. I close my eyes, inhaling air into my lungs only for my grief to steal it all away again before leaving me gasping silently. I will myself to keep the tears locked away.

I have cried too many times, wasted too many tears, and thrown away too much time.

"We should run." I speak to the ceiling, the words forcing from my throat in nothing but a choked whisper.

Along with the right to choose who I love, perhaps my father has also stolen my voice.

Although, as I realised when deciding to fight for Bash, he probably did that a long time ago.

If I had more energy, I would be angry with him again for letting society win over my happiness.

But I don't.

I am tired.

Fingers spread over my ankle, mattress dipping as his knees curled beneath him and his body shifts next to my own. He sighs, something sad, and it makes me want to turn my head. To find his lips and steal the next sad sigh from him before it reaches the world.

"What happened?" Bash asks quietly.

"They granted the license. It is done."

There is a sharpness to his whisper when he asks, "When?"

"A week."

Bash's hand finds mine, entwining our fingers, and this time my head does turn and my lips do meet his. Just as I said I would, I steal the sigh right from the depths of his lungs.

He pulls back, nipping gently at the bottom of my lip. I sigh and drag myself to the end of the bed. The black silk falls around me when I stand. My fingers rack through my hair. The ends are in knots that I will have to brush out later.

"We should have run weeks ago. I am foolish to think my father would choose me over society in the end." I say to myself more than to Bash.

He watches me, pulling himself to the edge of the bed and letting his elbows rest on his knees as his head drops into his hands. He's in the same pain I am. We are two halves of the same heart. Two people sharing the same soul now.

I should never have asked my mother to keep me back a year. I should never have fought against the feelings. I should never have believed that he didn't feel the same.

I spent so much time looking the other way. Procrastinating with the hopes things might change. I didn't need to.

Of course he felt the same.

I see it so clearly now.

It is written in the letters that are piled in a box in my wardrobe. It is in his eyes every morning that I descend the stairs to find him waiting for me. It is in his touch and in the way he kisses me. It is in the way I fit so perfectly against him.

God.

If only I hadn't waited.

"You will burn a hole in the carpet. Please stop," he asks as he watches me pace, the black fabric of my dress trailing behind. Our shadows are cast onto the walls, warped and flickering with the candle light.

"How can you be so calm?" I continue my pacing with my hands sitting heavily on my hips.

"Come here." He laughs as he holds a hand out.

"Stop laughing at me. You are so much more dramatic about much less." I take his hand and fall into his lap anyway. His fingers find my cheek and begin moving in a familiar pattern I've become accustomed to. My chest constricts and my brow furrows.

I cannot believe I will have to go without this.

I do not want to miss him. I do not want to know what missing him feels like.

But I also do not want to miss a moment of him so I do my best to shake off our impending heartbreak and look down at him. His messy dark hair is all over the place. His shirt is wrinkled. His hazel eyes shine. He is perfect.

I frown again as pain spreads from my heart and through my chest. Before I can rearrange my features, Bash catches the look.

"What is it?" he asks. I reach up to touch the fingers still caressing my face. My hand, soft and small, rests against his as I lean into his touch.

"I ... It's just I have become so used to you," I murmur and he smiles gently. "I will miss this."

The patterns stop as his hand presses gently into my cheek, turning my head toward him. He presses his lips to mine. "We will find a way."

"I know I said we should run, but I think ... I think it's too late for that now. Even though that would be the simplest way." I rest my forehead softly against his. "I think I might have to marry him."

He shakes his head, pulling back to catch my gaze. "Tils, you cannot—"

"Stop." I press my lips to his, silencing him. "I do not want to fight."

"Tilly ..." God. I will miss how he says my name. I move and lift to rest on my knees. I bunch the skirt of my dress in my hands as I settle my thighs over his. "What are you doing?"

Bash hasn't touched me again after that first night, against the tree and not far from a party full of polite society. The very memory of it still brings the heat to my cheeks and between my legs.

He kisses me each night as his fingers roam my body and become familiar with my curves. I memorise the pattern of his heartbeat as I lie on his chest, and I listen to the way his light snoring fills my bedroom.

But I crave the way he touched me that night in the small woods. I want more. I want all of him. I do not want to be dragged away against my will without experiencing this with him.

"I may have to marry him," I whisper, my fingers brushing lightly over the features of his face. "But I do not have to give him anything other than my hand. I want you to ... I need you to have me. All of me."

Chapter Thirteen

Tilly

Desire ignites and burns through me.

It rages under my skin as my hands fall down his chest, fingers toying and undoing each of the buttons of his cotton shirt. The fabric clings to his sculpted stomach. I suck in a breath as my fingers run over the hard muscle.

His hand covers mine and I look at him through heavy lashes. The hazel of his eyes darken to a molten gold.

"Are you certain?" he asks. The words are low and rough. An ache pulses within me and I shift in his lap. I roll my hips again and Bash groans, his hands sliding down my body and tightening on my hips.

The soft satin of my slip is soaked as it sticks to my thighs. My nipples are hard under the tight bodice of my corset. I feel like I am on fire and only Bash's hands on my body will help. I rest my forehead on his and shift closer to him on his lap.

His hands cup my face. He keeps my gaze as his fingers gently stroke my face. He looks into my soul. I feel as if one day he simply looked at me and I opened some door to him. I allowed him to take root in my heart and as time went on, I have felt him in every part of myself.

"Yes," I whisper.

He trails his fingers along a path down my neck, reaching around to pull out the few pins still in my hair. My red curls fall softly around my face and he tucks the strands behind my ears. He wraps his arms around my waist and stands, gently setting me to my feet. Still standing impossibly close, he kisses the corner of my mouth, my cheek, my forehead. I angle my face and stare up at him. He drops his lips to mine.

When he kisses me, my worries fade away.

We break apart and Bash turns me in his arms. His fingers work quickly to untie the cords in my corset. My hands hold it against my body as I feel it loosening.

"You are beautiful." His words wash over me as he murmurs into my ear. I feel the last cord loosen and I let my hands drop. The corset slides down my body as the silk fabric of the skirt falls to the ground. With the dress pooling at my feet, I turn back to face him.

He looks down my body. His eyes roam over my curves, the peaks of my nipples evident through my satin slip and he brushes a gentle thumb over one of them. A whimper falls from my lips and I arch into him. One of his hand snakes around my waist and the other lifts to brush the thin straps from my shoulders.

Bash presses gentle kisses across my shoulder and collarbone. I shiver under his touch.

"Bash," I whisper as his fingers gently tug my slip down my body. I gasp at the cool air washing over my skin as he exposes my breasts. I slide a hand over his shoulder to push the cotton shirt from his body.

"I dream about you," Bash murmurs. "Every night. Any time I close my eyes. But this ..." His hand brushes over my hips and the slip falls to the floor. He's shirtless, yet I stand naked in front of him. "This–*you* are perfection."

I smile at him, my body warm under his gaze. His hands on my waist, his fingers splaying over my skin. Safe. I am safe with Bash.

He pulls me closer to him, lifting my feet from the floor and spinning us. Gently, he lowers me onto the bed. I press my thighs together as I watch the way his throat moves as he swallows. His eyes do not leave my body. Mine do not leave his.

I lean back on my elbows and watch as he unties his trousers. The leather belt he wears drops on top of the pool of black silk. The fabric of his trousers slide over his thighs and my mouth dries.

I watch, wide eyed, as Bash drops a hand to his cock and pumps.

"You are ... That is ... Oh, God." I cover my face with my hands feeling the blush take over my face. Bash's gentle laugh soothes me as I feel his hand glide up my leg. His fingers hook under the tops of my stockings and roll them down, pulling them off my feet and adding them to the pile of our discarded clothes.

"Look at me, Tils," he says. His knee presses into the mattress as he crawls onto the bed, over me.

"I ... I don't know ..." I feel his lips press into my neck and I sigh. My hands leave my face and slip through his hair. Bash laughs softly and kisses me.

"Hey," he whispers, lips still on mine. "I love you."

I stare at him, watching his face before I surge forward and capture his lips again. This time it's with urgency. His hands grasp my waist and push me further up the bed. My head hits a pillow and Bash settles himself over me. My arms curl around his shoulders.

Bash's face looms over mine and shadows flicker around the room with the candlelight. He drops his lips to my skin and doesn't remove them. He leaves a hot trail across my collarbone and between the valley of my heaving breasts. He takes his time, rolling his tongue over my nipples and sucking them into his mouth.

I gasp and arch into him. He doesn't stop.

I drag my nails through his hair, down his neck. I feel like marking him. I feel like making him mine.

Bash moves down my body like he is an expert in it. I laugh softly as he drags his lips over my stomach and across my hips. As his mouth reaches the apex of my thighs, my eyes close. My fingers twist into his hair as his mouth closes around the bundle of nerves between my legs.

Behind the closed lids, our life seems to play out as if it were some performance on the stage I've gone to see. I can see him pulling me into him every morning. I can see us riding horses, swimming in the lake on the Archibald's Wescombe estate, walking in the gardens beneath the summer sun.

We would eat breakfast each morning, and then dinner each night, and every meal in between together. He would tell me about his day, or his recent business, or his latest adventure with Cassius and Freddy and I would listen, happy and content.

And then, when the sun goes down, and the stillness of night settles, we would do this.

I shiver and shake under his touch as he sucks and licks. My fingers tug at his hair as I squirm. I pant, and whimper, and try my hardest not to cry out.

So good.

It feels so good.

"Tilly?" Hearing my name on his lips causes me to shiver. I groan when he pulls away and crawls up my body. I miss the feeling of his mouth on me, of his hands gripping my thighs.

A part of me wants to examine them closely to see if he left any marks.

"You will tell me to stop? If I do not do it right or it hurts?" Bash hovers over me again as he settles himself between my legs.

"Vivienne said it would hurt. The first time," I reply, nodding and glancing down at our impossibly close bodies. His brow furrows and it makes me want to laugh. I lift a little to kiss him. "I will tell you. Promise."

He places a hand beside my head and lifts off my body. Instinct takes over and I reach between us. My fingers brush over his hard stomach before gently curling around his hard, weeping cock.

Bash hisses and I let go.

"No," he groans. Reaching down, he takes my hand and glides it back to his cock.

"It's so … big." I flex my fingers and then gently tug, mimicking the movement I'd watched Bash do only minutes ago. I memorise the look of him in my hand.

"You're good for my ego," Bash laughs, wrapping his fingers over mine and tightening our grip on him. I gasp as he tugs a little harder.

"I …" I swallow. "How is that … "

He smirks down at me before dropping another kiss to my lips. "It will fit."

Then Bash takes control.

He guides his cock to my entrance and slides the head through the wetness that's gathered between my thighs. He presses his forehead to mine as we both watch his movements.

"It will feel good. I promise," he murmurs. When I feel him drag the tip over my sensitive bundle of nerves, I gasp. He circles the top around my clit. At least, that's what Vivienne told me it was called. She didn't tell me it would feel this good.

"Ready?" Bash asks. I squirm beneath him, wanting more.

"Yes," I breathe.

He drags the head of his cock to find my opening again and slowly slips inside me. I gasp and adjust. There is pain, a dull ache that is ever present with all of his movements, but there is also pleasure. So, so much pleasure.

He starts slowly, pausing every few moments to take a deep breath, almost like he is steadying himself more than he is letting me adjust. Then he pushes further and further in. I hiss when he pushes gently through what feels like a barrier, and my eyes close as sharp pain radiates through me. Bash leans down and gently kisses me. He traces his tongue over my lips. He sucks my bottom lip into his mouth, nipping at it and drawing my attention from the pain.

When the worst of it subsides, I nod and he pushes all the way in.

Inch by inch, Sebastian Archibald fills me.

If we weren't already lost in one another before, there is now certainly no more hope. Breathy moans and quiet whimpers mix into one. The sounds twirl and intertwine. He drags himself out and then back in, slowly finding a rhythm. I gasp with pleasure everytime our hips find one another. Bash holds me tighter as he picks up his pace. Our lips meet over and over again.

There is no going back.

Not that I want to.

I am his. Utterly, entirely his. In this moment and in the next. In every single way that counts.

In my mind, in my heart, in my soul.

No marriage contract or an uncertain future can change that now.

Chapter Fourteen

Nora

"I swear that boy gets more and more disgusting each time I have to go in that room." The older maid coughs as my nose crinkles. "You are lucky the mistress doesn't allow the new maids into his rooms."

I give her a careful smile.

"I'm happy to swap with you for the afternoon. I'm sure I can handle it once, if you need a reprieve." It is a risk but my deadline is getting closer with every passing day and I've found, heard, seen, *nothing*.

The older maid sighs.

"Never you mind that. I've been here much too long now to know the suggestion would never fly with Mrs Krank. Even with the poor woman under stress from this ridiculous wedding."

"Surely, you … it's a wedding." I choose my words as carefully as I dare. My heart skips. "Is it not a happy occasion for the household?"

"Nothing happy is this much work," the older maid scoffs, pulling apart the stiff linens she took from Elliot Sinclair's rooms. I want to prompt her, want to get her to really talk. More than anything, I want my time in this house to be over sooner rather than later.

"I've never seen the bride. Is she nice?"

The older maid smiles, a little sadder than I expect for a servant of the groom's household.

"She isn't a regular guest. Never has been. She does have the most red head of hair. A bit blinding if you ask me." She shakes her head and heads out of the room. "Poor girl."

I sigh, left alone in the quiet room. The white shirt I'm mending slips through my light fingers, falling to the floor beneath the table.

"Bugger," I curse lightly. I push my chair back to reach under the table.

Voices drift into the room from the open door the older maid left through. I freeze, realising I am quite hidden beneath the dark, heavy table that runs the length of the small servants' dining hall.

"You make sure that the footman is well paid. We do not need anything else to go wrong before Sunday."

I close my eyes, listening hard.

"Yes, m'lady." That is Mrs Krank. Which means the other woman is …

"My son is an idiot, but this new wife of his is not. Unfortunately, she is annoyingly bright." It sounds as if Lady Sinclair scowls at the prospect of having an educated woman for a daughter-in-law. "She's charming, too. Would probably win over the servants with a smile. If anyone were to find out ..."

Lady Sinclair's voice fades as the two continue past the dining room and down the hall.

My heart races as I pull myself back into my chair.

Someone is being paid off.

Paid off to hide something.

But *what*?

This is a start. The tiniest glimmer of hope that there is a way. My hand itches, desperate to send the news to Lady Archibald but I hold myself in my seat.

The footman.

First, I will find him and get whatever secret he is hiding out of him. Then I shall tell Lady Archibald.

The cook tumbles into the room, arms full of bread and dishes of butter, so I go back to my mending while silently taking stock of the staff in this dismal house. With every stitch, I go over the names of the footmen in my head. One of them knows something and I am going to find out what it is.

If not for young Sebastian and his red-headed love, then for myself and the fresh air and bright corridors of Wescombe that I miss so dearly after the blackened walls of the Sinclair Residence and constant clouds of London.

CHAPTER FIFTEEN
BASH

Tuesday. Five Days Before The Wedding.

I WAKE TILLY SLOWLY on Tuesday morning.

It is early. The fog that normally takes an hour or two to clear with a new day's sun still hovers over the London houses. She hums as she shifts onto her back. My hands drift over her skin, my feather-like touch as soft and as promising as a new flower blooming in spring.

It is unwise to think about spring. Or anything past this summer season. Or anything past the coming Sunday, really.

It only ruins our moods. When I am with her, tucked away from the world and hidden beneath the sheets on her bed, I want her to forget about the grief that envelops us every other hour of every other day.

I want her to be here. Even if it's only behind the locked door of her bedroom. With me.

It will all end this Sunday with her walking toward another. Our time will then be up.

But it isn't yet.

Not yet.

I press warm kisses into the soft skin of her thigh, shifting my body down hers and settling between her legs.

The sigh that leaves her lips fills the room with an air of contentment.

Satisfaction.

My fingers are gentle as they dig into her hip, holding her in place as my tongue runs over her; again and again. With every press of my lips, every tease of my tongue, she feels as if I set her on fire. Embers fly until they finally catch and Tily is nothing but flames raging beneath me.

I stay here, watching her intently from my place between her legs, until she finally tugs at my hair. Her fingers twist deeply into my dark strands to get me to return my mouth to hers; where our lips move in sync, and fit perfectly, and taste just like her.

I roll us. Her knees fall either side of my hips, and she sinks down onto me. My groan gets lost in her mouth as she leans down to kiss me again. With my hands clutching her hips, I set the pace. She watches with wide eyes and her teeth buried into her bottom lip as I lose control. She matches my movements and desire burns through me. She sees it behind my golden hazel eyes as I watch her riding me. Watch her giving herself to me.

Her hand splays over my chest, balancing herself as she leans down. I dig my fingers into her hips, deeper and deeper. Here, right now in this moment, I know she'll let me do just about anything to her.

Her breasts press against my bare chest. Our bodies are flushed and glistening. She kisses me. I slow my hips to focus on her mouth, just for a second, and the change draws a whimper from the depths of her throat. I smirk.

Moving my lips down her neck and across her shoulder, I drag my teeth across her skin as I quicken my pace again.

"I love you," I whisper. "Forever. I need you to know that."

"I know you do," she murmurs back. Her words are gentle against my lips. "I love you, too."

"Do not forget." I thrust into her, earning another alluring whimper. "Never forget. Okay?"

"Yes." Her teeth dig back into her bottom lip. "I promise. Oh. *God*."

Not a night has passed since I first touched her in the small woodland by the lake, the moonlight streaming down on us through the canopy of branches above, that I haven't insisted on touching her; if only just by holding her in my arms. Since she gave me all of her, we have spent our evenings, our midnights, and our early mornings wrapped in one another.

Exploring, learning, listening.

My name remains her prayer; leaving her in whispers and whimpers.

I muffle my low, drawn out groan in her neck as her mouth hangs open in a silent scream. Tilly collapses against me, rolling off my body just in time for me to come on her thigh. Her chest heaves and her legs shake a little as they go limp over my own.

She tries to untangle herself from me but I reach out to stop her.

I want to keep her close. To keep her wrapped around me. While I can.

"We are getting very good at that," she breathes out, still trying to gulp down air.

"Don't," I shut my eyes tightly as she slips her arm across my waist. My body curls around hers, not caring about the mess I made on her thigh. "You cannot say things like that and then just expect me to be able to get up and go about my day."

"*You* are very good at that." Tilly kisses my collarbone, smiling. Her tone suggests she knows what she's doing.

"Ugh." I turn my head, eyes burning as I meet her gaze before tipping her chin with a finger and drawing her lips to mine. When I pull back a blush creeps over her face. "*You* are beautiful."

She hums, curling into me further. I push a loose piece of her hair behind her ear. Tilly sighs and her eyes close at my touch.

"Tell me about your day," she says.

She wants to listen to me talk. Just listen. The sound of my voice settles any nerves about her own day, about her own obligations that would see her having tea with Lady Sinclair and doing her best not to cry through it. She told me about it last night when I arrived. I held her to my chest as she cried.

And then we blocked out the world. We got lost in each other.

I suspect she wants to hear me talk for the same reason I always want to touch her. So that she can commit the sound of my voice and the way my slight Southern English accent curls around different words to her memory. I do the same with her Northern twinge.

"Do you want to talk about your day?" I ask softly, knowing her answer. She scrunches her nose and shakes her head. She won't talk about it again. Not now, not this week.

Not when Sunday looms closer and closer like a storm rolling in from the depths of the ocean.

"Okay. Well." I kiss her again, lips gentle on hers as I settle back into the pillows. "Cassius wants to go clay shooting this afternoon. But this morning I have a meeting with the ba—"

I cut myself off, cursing the slip. She raises a brow. "The—?"

"The bank," I finish.

Her brows pinch together and I can see her brain working to figure out why I wouldn't want to tell her that. I hold my breath, hoping that she will let it go.

She does not.

"Why do I feel like you are not just having a meeting with the bank?"

I know my guilt is written all over my face, and as if I extend it as a hand for her to take, the emotion reaches into her chest, wrapping around her lungs and squeezes as she realises.

"No. Bash. No, you mustn't."

"I have to try. I have to at least ask the question." I swallow. I watch her get momentarily distracted by the muscles in my neck flexing with the movement. My shoulders tense. Better to tell her the truth then keep it from her. That's not who we are. "I have a meeting with the banker in charge of the transaction and contract between your father and Lord Sinclair."

"You ... sorry?" Tilly pulls back, out of my arms, her hands gripping at the sheet and pulling it across her chest as she sits up.

"Tilly, don't ... come back here." I stare at her but she doesn't move. "Please."

"Why?"

"Tilly."

"Why, Bash?"

"I thought I might ... it depends on the terms and why Sinclair wants to get into your family business so badly but—"

I'm rambling. Tilly shakes her head and cuts me off with a stern tone. "Sebastian."

"I thought I might pay it." She blinks at me. Her fists clench tighter around the sheet she holds to her chest. I sit up, rubbing a hand over my jaw. "I could pay the contract out. Buyout Sinclair. Invest instead of ... then you wouldn't—"

"Bash, you cannot just buy me. I am not a piece of property or one of your business deals." Tilly raises her voice, leaning forward with her eyes wide.

"I know that."

"Do you? Because it sounds to me like you think simply throwing money at the problem will fix it."

"It will." This is not going to plan.

"No. It does not," she cries.

Tilly moves away from me, throwing her legs over the edge of the bed. She pulls on her silk robe that was forgotten on the floor last night and sits on the small stool to her dressing table.

"Do you not see how this would create a ridiculous imbalance. You would pay this contract, to marry me, to save me from that horrific, awful boy. I would be in your debt. We would not be starting our lives as equals and I—" She takes a breath, steadying herself. "I am scared that if you do this, you will end up resenting me for it. It is the same as running away and living a life outcasted from your family. What if ... what if this is not the fairytale we think it is ... what if we marry and move to the country and find that all we had was ... well, was physical?"

I stare at her, a look of utter confusion crossing my features. I wait a moment. Perhaps to see if she will start laughing, as if her comment is a hilarious joke between us that could never actually be fact.

When she doesn't begin to laugh, it sinks in that she is actually serious. "Tils."

She shakes her head. I see the tears form in her eyes before she drops my gaze. In the space of a heartbeat, I am off the bed and by her side.

"I'm sorry," I whisper as I drop to my knees in front of her. Her hands are buried in the folds of her dressing robe, but I reach to cover them with my own anyway. "I want to spend every moment of our lives with you. I want to wake up next to you, go to sleep by your side. I want to fill a house with children and then sneak away from them all so I can have you to myself every once in a while."

I reach up to catch one of the stray, salty tears falling down her cheeks.

"You are my best friend, the love of my life. How can that be just sex."

Finally, she laughs. It's breathless and broken but it's still a laugh. I revel in the sound like it's the first sun after a month of cloud and rain.

"Cassius will be so very upset I have stolen his title," she whispers through a watery smile.

"It is yours to take. It has always been yours." I reach up and stroke a thumb over her cheek. "Tils. Even if you changed your mind and told me tomorrow that you did not love me and you did not want to marry me, I would still want to pay it. I want you to be happy. That's it. The only thing I want to acquire from that deal is your happiness. With me or otherwise."

Chapter Sixteen
Bash

Wednesday. Four Days Before The Wedding.

I hate smoking.

Cigars, cigarettes, any of them.

The smell makes my stomach churn and I hate the way the taste of them hangs about in the air for days. My head pounds and the whiskey always tastes a little off when there is smoke in the air. The smooth amber liquid never quite burns in the same satisfying way it usually does. I hate it.

My eyes narrow as Cassius balances a cigarette between his teeth, pulling a box of matches from his pocket. He cups a hand around the end of the white stick, lighting it, inhaling and then exhaling as he adds to the already copious amount of the disgusting substance milling around the room.

I cough, albeit weakly, eyes focusing on the culprit that sits idly between Cassius' fingers.

"Sod off, Archibald," he says in a bored tone.

"Do you have to fucking do it inside?" I snap back, thankful Cassius took the bait. I'm itching for a reason to fight, to bicker, to snap.

Yesterday had started fine—more than fine, truthfully, much more—but ended in me storming from the bank, the black clouds above following me home.

I swirl the glass of cigarette flavoured whiskey in my hand, wrist rotating slowly as the ice slides around the edges of the glass. My thoughts go back to the darkened office.

Long afternoon hours wasted pouring over paper; the ledger, the reports, the statements, and, as much as I wanted to throw up seeing a copy in person, the investment contract that had used Tilly—my Tilly—as a commodity.

My own banker, Kennedy, gave up long before I did. He threw down his quill and declared there was simply no loophole to be found. The documents were sound.

Completely legal.

The anger hasn't quite subsided, the rain and the storm that rolled through London worsening my sour mood as the evening wore on. I made excuses for myself at the Christoph's Anniversary Party last night and left mere minutes after arriving. I had watched as Tilly shrunk behind her mother before being tugged by the arm to stand in front of Elliot Sinclair. Her father stood next to her, hand still tightly wrapped around her upper arm, looking proud.

It made me sick.

Sinclair looked bored at first, like he was completely uninterested in Tilly. Then he spotted me watching them over her shoulder. He smiled and winked, before leaning toward her, whispering to her even as she flinched away from him. Elliot looked so pleased with himself when the glass in my hand had shattered and I excused myself from the ballroom.

I'd been tempted to take my anger out of a few more of my mother's plates and vases when I'd arrived home but resisted.

She had yet to forgive me for the last few.

One of the servers replaces my glass but I don't lift my eyes and merely nod in thanks.

I stare at the fresh glass placed in my hand. It's crystal.

Delicate. Hand crafted.

Breakable.

A familiar ache spreads through my chest. Tilly and I are mere crystals.

Delicate and hand crafted and, come Sunday, breakable.

If it weren't for the immense pain in my chest, I might be tempted to laugh. By the end of this week, Tilly and I will be mere pieces of something that once was beautiful and unique but is now shattered and destroyed.

I will have to eventually figure out how to fix things. Figure out how to sweep up the fragments so that I become a neat, little pile. Ready to be put back together.

Although, I am not entirely sure whether it will be worth it.

What future lay ahead of me that doesn't involve her?

"Come on, Archibald. It will be alright," Cassius says to bring me back from my own thoughts. He drags on the cigarette through his teeth, lips forming a tunnel when he exhales into the air. "Sinclair won't live forever. You might get lucky. A bout of fever might get him early."

"Cass." Freddy growls as the book in his hands lowers.

My eyes drop back to my glass still idly grasped between loose fingers.

It's a nice weight. Heavy and expensive. A signature used for their drinks at the club. For a moment, I think about letting it go. I think about watching it also shatter into a thousand little pieces. Perhaps if I throw enough vases against enough walls, or allow enough glass tumblers to slip through my fingers, I might find one that doesn't break, that doesn't shatter, and it might give me hope that Sunday may not completely ruin me after all.

There is no drop, no slip.

Nothing but a defeated sigh and a pounding headache.

"It was never about the money. He wanted the boats, and the name, and her," I say quietly.

"I wasn't even aware Sinclair knew who she was," Freddy replies, fiddling with the pages of his book.

"He didn't, but he does now. Bash made sure of that," Cassius answers for me.

My head snaps up, my fingers still holding the glass tightening as I stare at Cassius. "What the fuck, Montgomery?"

"Oh, come on." Cassius glances back and forth between Freddy and I, mouth curling into a smirk. "Mate, it's not like you have tried to hide it. Both of you. Even before you went all soft for her. He—*everyone*—knows that you two are insane about each other. You two have always been like this."

"Shove off. We haven't always." I glare at him.

"I've got to agree with Cass on this one." Freddy turns the book over in his hands. "Sinclair is only a few years older than us. He's good mates with Tallbot who was at school with us. We are not exactly introverted people."

I throw back the rest of my whiskey, blistering my throat as it burns. I grimace and lean forward to rest my arms on my knees. My head drops as I spin the glass in my fingers. "I can't do a fucking thing."

"Bash." Freddy tosses the book onto the small table between us. He levels with me, reaching to grasp my shoulder. "You cannot think—"

"Well, well, well." The drawl is familiar and it feels like ice sliding down my spine. "Look who it is, Gregory. The competition."

Elliot Sinclair takes two stairs at a time, shrugging off his coat jacket as he rounds on our small table. His eyes sparkle with amusement and it makes me see red. I inhale, immediately regretting it when my head pounds hard as the taste of smoke swirls in my mouth.

My knuckles go white against the glass as I meet Sinclair's eyes. I don't miss the lurking figure of Gregory Tallbot a few paces behind Sinclair. He nods at us and his mouth pulls into a tight line.

"Fuck off, Sinclair," Cassius says in his bored tone again. The mask of Lord Montgomery slips across his features as he pulls the men's attention.

Gratitude tightens around my lungs. Cassius knows Sinclair's type better than any of us. He shared the first half of his childhood in nurseries surrounded by them after all. I don't miss the slight smirk that tugs at the edge of Cass' mouth as he raises his chin, cigarette still hanging between his fingers as he adds on, "Respectfully."

"Not to worry, Montgomery. Thought I'd just extend an invite to the big day on Sunday." Sinclair's words drip with amusement. The pain already digging into my chest sharpens and I will myself not to let my face show any emotion. "Although, I think I'm looking forward to Sunday night more."

Anger boils under my skin, prickling at my nerves and when I meet Sinclair's smug look I launch forward.

Cassius and Freddy are with me, mirroring my movements as they stand from their seats. But they move between Sinclair and I. Freddy pushes on my shoulder and Cassius furiously shakes his head. The glass finally slips from my fingers to the oak floor.

A single crack splinters the tumbler into two pieces left abandoned at my feet.

Sinclair's biting laughter slides down my spine as my foot knocks one half of the glass, pulling my gaze and my attention for a moment.

In the quiet moments as we are admired from afar, Tilly and I look beautiful and reflective and one of a kind.

But with every rising sun the existing cracks run deeper while new ones appear. It will only take one touch. A mere ghost of a touch and we will shatter. Just as crystal does. Once glittering and impressive as a whole, we will be nothing.

Breakable.

Elliot Sinclair is that one touch.

My vision blurs and in the depths of my mind the memories of Tilly reel. Except it isn't me that holds her, kisses her, makes her smile, makes her laugh.

It is Sinclair.

That reality blurs and I watch her fall into his touch, her gaze softening as she looks at Sinclair just as she does me when she reaches to run a gentle hand through his hair instead of mine. Jealousy and rage and disgust courses through me as I push the images away.

Tilly would never, will never, look at Sinclair like that.

I meet Sinclair's smug gaze.

Cass discards his cigarette butt on the table as his hand steadies against my shoulder.

"Bash ..." Cass' swaps his bored tone for a warning one. I ignore him, still glaring at Sinclair. I very much want to rearrange the smug bastard's face. "Bash. Not here."

"Yes, Bash. Not here." Sinclair's smile widens. "Wouldn't want people getting the wrong idea ... you're so protective. I wonder why ..."

"I think it's time for you to go, Sinclair. You have made your point," Freddy says. My friend stands in front of me blocking me from moving.

"It's okay that you have had her, Archibald. I don't mind," Sinclair says as he steps in. Freddy pushes him back, a hand in the centre of his chest, roughly shoving him off course. "That way when you see us together, you'll remember what she sounds like. What she feels like, tastes like. You'll remember that I took her from you. I am going to ruin her."

Cassius' hand drops from my shoulder. The pressure holding me back alleviates and, when Freddy steps aside, the path between me and Sinclair's smug face is clear.

I sink my right fist deep into his jaw.

The crunch of a bone echoes as silence falls over the room's occupants. My head still pounds, the smoke lingering in the air still fogging up my mind, and scratching my throat with every breath. I shake out my hand.

Fuck that hurt.

"You bastard." Sinclair spits blood onto the oak floor.

"You will not touch her," I growl. I step back, catching one half of the cracked glass beneath my boot. It splinters once more.

"You don't get a say. She is marrying me, Archibald. She will be mine to do with as I please," he says, grinning and showing his blood stained teeth. I want to punch him again.

"I got there first. I remember watching her be presented for the first time. We all knew she was pretty, but her family aren't as wealthy as some others. Her dowry is not as large, even if that business of Prescott's could be somewhat profitable in the right hands." Sinclair flexes his fingers, indicating that the hand he speaks of is his own.

I bite down on the feeling rising in my chest as I'm over-whelmed by the strong urge to break his jaw properly.

"Gregory was interested. Weren't you Greg?" Sinclair throws a glance back at the hovering form of Gregory Tallbot. He turns back to me, the smile on his face turning salacious. "But so were you. That much was blatantly obvious. It was too easy and I was bored. I told my father that he should look at investing in Prescott's small trading business. He is been moving to take a majority in the trade market lately. A little project of his. Slipping in the idea that he should propose a match, have the investment sealed with a binding, legal marriage? Well ... even my father admitted it was a stroke of genius."

"This is all a game to you?" My throat burns.

"I suppose so. Look at that. I won." Sinclair wipes a hand across his mouth, spreading a streak of blood from his cheek to his ear.

"I won't let you. You won't use her as a part of your sick games," I say.

We will run.

We will have to now. Once I tell Tilly about this, she will surely agree.

She is a good rider. We could ride through the night. Perhaps, with a bit of help from my parents, we might get a boat. Leave completely. Go to the colonies. Whatever puts distance between Tilly and the monster that is pushing her around like a piece on a chess board for fun. For his own entertainment. As if she is something disposable.

"It's too late, Archibald."

Silence descends on the room and I feel as if the air has been sucked from my lungs.

The blood has dried across Sinclair's face. My knuckles are beginning to bruise and my hand throbs.

The glass at my feet still sits splinted but not yet shattered at my feet.

"I challenge you to a duel—" My face is set. My features slide into a hard mask and my shoulders stiffen. Freddy's head, previously eyeing Gregory wearily, snaps to me. Cassius' smile curls across his face and he shakes his head, amusement evident in the roll of his eyes. "—Friday."

"You're insane, Archibald. They're illegal," Gregory finally says, speaking from his spot on the outskirts of the fray. I pay little attention to him with my hard gaze still set on Sinclair who has begun to regard me with a mix of intrigue and wonder.

Gregory takes another step, hand on a knife that none of us noticed he had pulled out. Cassius moves into his path, snarling and shoving him backwards.

"This doesn't concern you, Tallbot," Cass spits out.

Gregory slinks away from Cassius looking as if his deepest desire is to sink the knife he holds into Cassius' neck.

"You're scared you'll lose, Sinclair?" I force myself to keep my voice steady; the image of complete conviction.

"No. Unlike you, I have held a pistol for more than clay shooting." Sinclair cocks his head to the side and I feel the urge to knock the amusement off his face with another right hook. "You must really love her if you are willing to die for her."

I hold his gaze. I rise to my full height and jut my chin out but say nothing.

"Okay, Archibald. You can have your duel." Sinclair holds out his hand. "Friday. Sunset. And ... no doctor. One will win. The other will die."

I look at the hand Sinclair holds out to me, fingers tinged red from the blood he swiped from his busted lip and nose. I take it.

"Gregory will be my second. Don't see why we should involve anyone else in our little illegal duel."

"Cassius will be mine." I shake on it.

Sinclair nods. The amusement still clings to his features and drips from the corners of his mouth. Our hands still clasped together, Sinclair pulls hard and forces me to step in. He smiles in my face. "Make sure you kiss her hard and long, Archibald. It will be the last time you ever do."

I rip my hand away and flex my fingers. Sinclair's biting laughter rings out, echoing as they retreat. I am left standing and staring after them; fingers bruised, features set, shoulders stiff.

The tumbler in two beneath my feet is proof that not all glass shatters. Sometimes, it merely splinters.

Could a splinter be fixed with a pointed pistol and one well-aimed bullet?

I hope so.

"What the fuck are you playing at?" Freddy's hard whisper cuts through my trance.

"What is there to lose, Fred? By Sunday I will have lost everything anyway. She does not want to run, she won't let me pay. If I kill him ... "

"If you kill him, you become some other man. The Bash I know—the Bash that Tilly loves—wouldn't kill anyone." Freddy stares at me, light blue eyes sharper than a dagger as it cuts into my whiskey coated resolve. "Do not do it this way."

"There is no other way." I drop back into the armchair, reaching for the splintered pieces of the glass tumbler. "At least this way I get the chance to put a bullet in him first."

Cassius laughs, clapping me on the back with his eyes shining.

"Cass, this isn't funny. Duels are illegal. With no doctor present one of you *will* die," Freddy pleads.

"Lighten up, Fred." Cassius swings one leg over the other, stretching his arm across the back of the chaise he sits on. He fumbles in his breast pocket before pulling out another cigarette and placing it between his teeth. "Besides. They will do as gentlemen do and aim for the sky. Won't you, Bash?"

I can't answer him.

Won't.

"Then, we'll talk it out like fucking adults and find out what Sinclair wants more than Tilly," he continues, oblivious to my blank stare and reeling mind. Cassius lights the cigarette. Inhaling and exhaling, the air around us clouds with smoke again.

That would be the gentlemanly thing to do.

To count my ten steps and then aim for the sky. Only then, once the smoke from the gunpowder clears, will we cross the field and speak of money and bribes and whatever else it may take to get Sinclair to give me what I know he doesn't want.

It is how every other duel is settled. Between disgruntled brothers or untrustworthy foes. A gentleman would aim for the heavens.

Still, I cannot answer. I will have Elliot Sinclair at the end of my pistol. In my line of sight.

Will aiming at the sky be an option once I stare at him down the barrel of a gun?

Chapter Seventeen
Tilly

Thursday. Three Days Before The Wedding.

Time slides through my fingers.

My days pass in a blur of wedding plans. I was the little girl that loved weddings. The dresses, the jewels, the happiness. I longed for my own. I imagined it time and time again. Never in my wildest dreams did I ever imagine that I would be wishing for it all to be over. To end.

By Thursday, I long for nightfall and the comfort that his arms bring me. Time slows and comes to a stop when he wraps me up in his orbit. I relax into his touch. I sigh into his kiss. He surrounds me and blocks out the rest of the world.

Bash is quiet this evening.

He presses his face into my neck when he joins me in bed, having slipped off his shoes after locking the door. My hand buries into his hair, scraping my nails gently across the back of his neck and through his messy strands. I feel his mouth press gently against my throat. He's soft at first. Slow and careful.

I twist my fingers further into his hair and Bash lifts his head to find my waiting lips.

We take our time.

He holds my gaze. My attention. He kisses me more and more. When we fall, we fall together.

Bash rests his forehead against mine. I listen to his hard breathing as I catch my own breath. He doesn't move from above me. I stroke his cheek with a single finger and try to coax him to look at me.

He pulls back and blinks. The pain in his eyes is as clear as day.

I tuck myself into his side and stay quiet. My fingers trace patterns on his now bare chest. I try to pour the love I have for him through my touch.

I listen to his shallow breathing as darkness takes a hold on the room around us. I think about finding a candle to light, desperate to search his eyes so I can figure out what he is thinking.

Eventually, he speaks into the darkness. "Do you think you will ever love him?"

"Maybe," I say, my words a mere whisper. "In another life, I might have."

The moon comes out from behind a cloud and the room illuminates. Bash's eyes are trained at the ceiling. I sigh.

"When I was a girl, I dreamt about my wedding every day. I thought about the flowers, the music, and the food. I would picture what sort of dress I might wear. I knew I wanted a diamond ring just like my mother's. I was naive and young and in love with the idea of getting married." I swallow, the familiar tug of tears sitting just behind my eyes. "I never, never, pictured the man I would marry. He was faceless when I was younger. And I was happy with that, content with the faceless man if it meant I got all the other stuff."

It is so quiet I can hear him swallow. As the air seems to thicken, everything else simply fades away. Darkness presses in. It is as if we are in the middle of an ocean, floating in the calm waters as a storm rages all around us.

We are the eye.

"And now?" he asks.

"I still picture all of those things; the white dress, the flowers, the food." My eyes close even though I can barely see in the dark. I trace over his heart. My heart. The one I own. As he owns mine. "He isn't faceless anymore. Hasn't been for a long time."

The fingers that are weaved into my hair still. The shoulder that I tucked myself into shudders.

"Who do you see?"

It is too much.

I can see his happy, handsome face as he smiles at me from across a ballroom or on the street or in the park clearly in the darkness. But my heart breaks because I hear the whispered and cracked words coming from him now and the smile fades.

Does he really not know?

All of it hurts. We are painted in the pain that has haunted us since the night in my father's office when he kissed me and told me he loved me and asked me to marry him.

"You know who," I whisper back.

"Can you … I need you to say it." His fingers tighten in my hair, the gentle pressure tilting my head and pulling my face toward his. "Please."

The moonlight, a mere sliver of bright reflection, streams through my bedroom window. As my eyes adjust to the low light, I catch the glass-like a tear that slides from his eye.

"I picture you. I pictured you when I was twelve and missed you so dearly I thought I'd be lost without you. I pictured you every time I got one of your letters. I pictured you every time you stood at the bottom of the stairs at the house with that stupid grin. Every single day since the day you told me you loved me too, I have pictured you."

I push myself off his shoulder, my hand pressing into the mattress to keep myself steady as I slide a leg across his body and settle myself above him. My fingers dance over his jaw, tracing down the lines of his neck, over his shoulders and back again. They find themselves in his hair before I speak again, leaning down to press my lips against another of the escaped tears on his cheek.

"You would have to not exist for me to love another. From the moment our parents threw us together, it was done. That was it."

"We were four," I hear the smallest of chuckles in his voice and the sound makes my heart sing.

"When you know, you know."

"Tils."

"I was made for you, Sebastian Archibald." I brush my lips against his. "And you were made for me."

I feel him smile, his lips pulling upward and dragging against my own. I kiss him, sighing into his mouth as his hands find my waist. When he pulls back, he brushes his nose against mine, fingers digging into my skin like he's afraid I might try to move away.

As if I would ever want to leave his arms.

"I love you," he murmurs. "In every life. This and the next."

The words slip from his tongue and settle in my chest. I am weighed down, something prickling at my nerves as he holds me so closely. Something that feels as if it will soon weave through my nightmares with vigour.

It feels as if he is saying goodbye.

Friday. Two Days Before The Wedding.

The satin sits heavy on my body. It hugs my chest and warms my skin as the seamstress flitters around me with pins sticking out from between her teeth. I run my fingers over the beading, my breathing shallow as I close my eyes briefly.

The dress—with its long train and tightened waist, white as snow and a perfect fit for something that we only ordered days ago—is the perfect dress. The bright white contrasts the burning red of my hair, and my eyes sting when I eye the barely visible and fading purple mark just beneath my left ear.

The right dress, the wrong man.

Not for the first time this week, I swallow my tears in public as I wish with everything that I am that I could disappear or that the ground might open up and finally allow me to fall through it. I cannot for the life of me understand why I didn't insist the window coverings be shut. Those passing by get a front row view of my misery.

As another group of nosy mothers gawk at me through the window, I wonder if I am being stared at and pitied because they know I am in love with another, or because Elliot Sinclair's reputation is truly atrocious.

The difference is minimal. I deserve their pity.

I shudder through another heavy sigh and will myself to hold my head up.

I catch another glance of myself in the mirrors. The seamstress sits on her knees at my feet as she tugs at the fabric. There are deep set shadows beneath my eyes, my skin is pale, my normally bright green iris' dull. I suddenly wish I hadn't shooed my mother away at the beginning of the fitting. I feel as if I need someone else here to reaffirm that this dress and the event it represents is a mere single day in my life and not the final nail in my closing coffin.

A coffin that has been sealing me in since the day my father signed his name next to the devil's and offered me up as payment.

Dramatics.

I hear the word in his voice, echoing around my head and hurting my heart. I bite down on my bottom lip in an attempt to subdue the sob that rolls up my throat.

As a little girl, I danced around our nursery with Florence. Much to Baggins' dismay, we stripped the white sheets from our already-made beds and wore them as wedding gowns. We used the long corridors of the Prescott country house to practice our slow march down an imaginary aisle and we took it in turns to lead each other in a messy, incorrect waltz.

Our laughter filled the halls then, our friendship solid in sisterhood and the reality that marriage was still a lifetime away.

Five years ago, I watched Florence cling to our father's arm with determination written all over her features as she finally made the journey down the aisle, white dress and pink flowers in hand. I watched as my sister stood in front of a man twice her size while she promised to love and to obey him. She wore a look of stern acceptance of her own fate, the same that she wore when she asked our parents to find her match in the first place.

Florence hadn't waited. Hadn't wanted to, she'd said, and was married within months of her first season.

I sat between Vivienne and Bash at the wedding, my fingers curled into his and hidden in the folds of my dress as he comforted me. I was upset that my sister hadn't wanted me to stand with her. Even then, before I knew what the butterflies in my stomach meant and brushed off the dreams he frequented as nothing, I leant on him for comfort and for support in the hardest of times.

The seamstress steps back, her lips purse and the fabric slips easily through her fingers as she fans out the train of the dress behind me.

I follow the line of the train, my eyes gazing effortlessly over my own figure in the mirror. I imagined the skirt to be fuller, more structured. Like Florence's. A princess ball gown. The fabric hanging off me feels as if it weighs a ton but it falls easily and in effortless waves.

It cinches at a hand stitched corset that accentuates my thin waist. My breasts are pressed so tightly into the bodice they threaten to spill over. When I take a breath, the dress rises and falls in time.

The seamstress clicks her tongue, snapping my attention toward her and holds up a handkerchief. I stare at her confused until she shakes the fabric at me. Only then do I touch a finger to my own cheek. I feel the dampness and when I look up at my face in the reflection, I realise I have begun to cry.

I didn't even notice.

I take the handkerchief from the seamstress and do my best to smile convincingly at her.

A small bell chimes from the front of the store. I duck my head to wipe the tears from my cheeks, closing my eyes. I work on steading myself as I count to ten and try to regain my composure.

The right dress.

The wrong man.

"Whatever the circumstances, you make a beautiful bride, my dear." A familiar voice speaks softly from across the shop. My eyes fly up and meet the older woman's gaze. Eleanor doesn't have the exact colour of her son's eyes—a hazel that dips in gold with the sunlight or melts into a bronze heat in the evenings—but they are similar enough for my walls to fall. With them go the flood of tears that I have been holding back ever since being dragged to the atelier this morning for this final dress fitting.

"I'm sorry," I sob, sinking to my knees. The dress flows out around me. It is a sea of white satin and only reminds me that I am moments from drowning in some twisted version of what is supposed to be my very own fairytale.

"Close those curtains." Eleanor's voice is sharp, commanding, but I can only press my face into the borrowed handkerchief. A soft touch brushes the curls from my shoulder, tracing down my chin until a hand rests against my cheek. "Breathe, Matilda. Breathe."

"It is all wrong," I sob.

"I know, dear."

"It is not supposed to go like this—" the words catch in my throat. I shake my head, my eyes filling with tears again. Eleanor is patient as she shifts some of the fabric away, making some space to sit next to me on the raised platform. I curl into the elder woman's side. "I have not cried this much in my entire life. I ... I am sad all the time."

"Your wedding is supposed to be a happy day," she responds, stroking my hair softly.

"Were you happy on your wedding day?"

"Deliriously so."

I smile softly, the look on Eleanor's face reminding me of Bash whenever I catch him looking at me. Neither of us speak, a knowing silence falling between us as she continues running a gentle hand over my hair. The seamstress disappears and I can hear the sound of ripping fabric muffled through the wall. I smooth a hand across the corset of the dress again, the boning digging into my skin.

"It's a beautiful dress, Matilda. You are stunning in it. If it is worth anything, there won't be a single eye that does not follow you the entire way down that aisle," Eleanor says quietly.

"It ... it is the perfect dress." I take a deep breath, pulling my head from Eleanor's shoulder. My words tremble as they fall from my mouth before I can catch them. "Do you think he would like it?"

"Oh, Tilly ..."

Neither of us need to speak his name aloud. We both know whose opinion I truly want.

I shake my head again, vision blurring as the tears glaze over my eyes. I blink them away, pulling myself from Eleanor's grasp and standing again.

I begin to tug at the sleeves, trying to pull the dress from my body. I need to shred the satin that hugs my curves perfectly, flows from my waist elegantly, and moves as if it breathes with me.

It is all too much.

Eleanor abandons the small bag she holds on the ground, steps behind me and pushes my hair away from the delicate buttons that hold the fabric taunt against my chest. I feel her pull at the hidden cords of the corset, my chest falling as the bodice drops to the floor. My chest feels lighter, the gown crumpling at my feet, yet it becomes clear as I try to fill my lungs that it hadn't been the dress, hadn't been the tight corset or the soft satin.

It is the right dress, but the wrong man.

Chapter Eighteen
Tilly

Eleanor catches me, pulling me into her chest and cradling me as if I were her own. She strokes a hand through my long hair smoothing out the curls and rubs soothing circles against my back. Eventually, when my eyes dry and are left red and itchy, Eleanor passes me my soft green dress to change into.

"I'm sorry," I apologise.

"They say it's healthy to cry, even if you have been told your entire life that it is not." She gives me a small smile, lifting a finger to brush lightly against my cheek.

Eleanor is a mother.

She is soft and kind, calm in the face of extreme emotion and understanding beyond reason in matters that would otherwise seem trivial. She cares for the children that grace her life and it matters very little what their last name is or how their presence in her life has come to be.

I have seen it in the way she loves Freddy and Cassius as her own.

She is also fierce, and confrontational, and fights for what she believes in. I admire her immensely, always stunned when she speaks to whoever about whatever she pleases. Eleanor has opinions. Real opinions. On things like politics, science and industry. She is educated and has a voice. She fights for her family without pause and with vigour.

She fought for Bash, and lately she has fought for me, too.

"You've been … so kind. To me." I drop my eyes, staring at the shoes I've just slipped my feet into. "Even though I'm hurting your son. I'm sorry."

"Matilda." Eleanor taps a finger under my chin, silently asking me to meet her gaze again. "You are not hurting Bash. You are hurting *with* him. And for that, I am truly sorry."

My hands are gathered between Eleanor's, held tightly as the hazel eyes I know so well swirl with worry. She searches my face as if trying to find a way into my head, my heart, to calm and soothe me further.

"Neither of you deserve to experience such heartbreak before you truly have a chance to love and to be loved properly."

There is nothing for me to say.

I agree, of course I do.

Bash and I barely began before we've been forced apart. We have been inches from one another, close enough to see the future we could have, before it all has gone completely and utterly wrong.

"Will you come for tea?" Eleanor asks.

I blink. "Tea?"

"Yes. Tea. With me. I do believe the cook can probably rustle up some biscuits for us but knowing my husband, she probably has already." Eleanor begins to move, gathering her things and standing.

"I—Yes, of course."

The stifling summer air follows us through the streets of London and into the Archibald's comfortable drawing room. With a note of my whereabouts sent to my mother, the invitation to join us conveniently left out, I slip off my shoes and curl my legs beneath myself on one of the settees.

I watch Eleanor push open the windows, allowing a soft breeze to filter through the room. She is busy tying back curtains when Mrs Michaels walks in with the tea tray.

"My Lady." The housemaid tuts. "You should've let me."

"No need, no need. I can manage just fine." Mrs Michaels holds a disapproving expression as she pours my tea. Eleanor sits next to me, accepting her own cup from Michaels. "See. Now we have the tea and the breeze. Teamwork."

She throws me a wink as the housekeeper leaves the room, mumbling under breath about duties of a Lady. My eyes close as I bring the tea to my lips, my body relaxing into the cushions as the hot liquid slides down my throat. The Archibalds keep their home comfortable, warm, and inviting. They rarely throw society events in their actual home, choosing locations like museums or the boat houses for anything they have a hand in. They are private, and quiet, and they were almost mine.

It makes my chest ache thinking about it. About how I might have been a part of it, might have been enveloped into the same love and care that Cassius and Freddy, even Vivienne, had been.

As Eleanor keeps me entertained with stories of her and Harold's worldly travels, I feel the knot in my stomach loosen. The heavy weight on my chest lifts and as I laugh with my head thrown back and my tea cup shaking a little in my hand, I realise that Eleanor set out to make me forget about the dress, and the wedding, and the wrong man for as long as she can manage it.

Appreciation for Bash's mother floods through me.

"You must go to Greece one day but only in May or September, otherwise it is much too hot or too cold. Harold once—" Eleanor breaks off at the sound of a knock. The door of the drawing room pushes open before she has the chance to answer.

For a moment I am afraid it may be my mother coming to drag me away.

Or worse, my father.

A housemaid rushes into the room. Eleanor stands and meets her in the middle of the room, taking the housemaid's hand in hers. I cock my head to the side and drown slightly, noticing the housemaid is dressed differently to the others in the household. Strange.

"I am so sorry to interrupt, m'Lady." The woman's eyes run over me and I shift under her curious gaze, heat rising up the back of my neck. "But I came as soon as I was able to get away. I—"

The housemaid pauses, casting me another hesitant glance. Eleanor shakes her head.

"Come in, Nora. It is quite alright. This is Matilda Prescott," Eleanor introduces me and understanding floods the maid's features. "So you are more than welcome to speak freely in front of her."

I don't miss the way Nora's eyes sadden as she looks over at me before she squares her shoulders. There is a pause. Goosebumps rise on my skin. The air tastes like anticipation as Eleanor nods for Nora to give her the urgent news.

"Elliot Sinclair has gotten Charlotte Ravenswood pregnant."

The curtains bristle in the light breeze and the ticking of a clock that sits on the mantle amplifies.

You could hear a pin drop.

The maid still stands in the middle of the room with her hands in Eleanor's. Her gaze flickers between Eleanor and I.

My heart thuds.

Pregnant.

Elliot has gotten Charlotte pregnant.

God.

"You are certain?" Eleanor all but whispers.

"Yes. Absolutely. The housekeeper was complaining about having to plan a wedding in such a short time and that Elliot isn't helping with his actions. Apparently your Mrs Baggins has given her quite the hard time, turning up unannounced." Nora gives me a kind smile as if she hopes the knowledge that my housekeeper has been difficult will make me feel better about all this. "But I am certain. Charlotte bribes one of the footmen to let her in after dark."

I focus on Nora as something floods my chest, swirling around my lungs before tightening.

Shame.

I am no better than Charlotte Ravenswood. No better than Elliott. Allowing Bash to stay with me each night after passing a small purse of shillings to my own footman to keep our secret.

Suddenly, with a shiver down my spine and the air draining completely from my lungs, I press a hand over my stomach. Terror mixes with something else. Something that grapples with my mind and my logical thought process.

Excitement.

Maybe even ... hope.

"And you took everything with you? You didn't leave anything behind?" Eleanor questions. When I glance up at her, she's smiling. Her eyes are bright and shining with elation. With victory.

"Yes, m'Lady. I left a note for the housekeeper that I was returning home to care for an ill parent at once. She will have no reason to expect otherwise. It is not as if they bothered to look too closely at me when I began there anyway," Nora explains.

"Good. You must return to Wescombe at once. I hate to think how Lord Sinclair will react when the society learns of his son's misdemeanour." Eleanor nods, more to herself than to Nora or I. "I will call for the country carriage to be pulled around. You must go. Today."

"M'lady, I—" Nora shifts between her feet nervously. "I ran into some of the other housemaids on my way here, and I thought ... I thought it would be best if perhaps it didn't come from Michaels. If it is traced back to you or to m'Lord, they could try to accuse you of lying to stop the wedding."

Silence falls again and I realise both women are staring at me.

A finger curls into the fabric covering my stomach and my insides churn. Images of a small, tiny baby, with ten fingers and ten toes and a mop of messy black hair forms in my mind.

"Matilda?" Eleanor touches a hand to my arm gently to draw my attention. When I look up, I realise Nora is gone. "Are you ... are you upset about this news?"

I blink at her.

"No, I ..." I hesitate wondering whether I should tell her about what Bash and I have been doing. I chew on my bottom lip, fingers still pressing into my stomach. The last thing I want to do is disappoint Eleanor.

She returns to sitting by my side and reaches for the hand pressing to my stomach.

"I am sure that Sebastian, as reckless and careless as he is at times, will have been more careful with you. He knows—well, Cassius knows and I am certain they will have spoken—how to ensure nothing comes of your premarital activities."

"You know?" I say meeting her amused gaze.

"Bash has never had a knack for stealth. Not like Cassius, anyway. It took me months to figure out that he was disappearing to sleep in another bed when he lived under this roof." Eleanor smiles as she pats my hand gently.

"You're not ... angry with me? With us?"

"God no. I can hardly blame the two of you." She laughs. "Harold was the same when I was your age. He would find a way to get what he wanted, regardless of the risks."

I blush to the same colour as my hair, but I smile and lift my free hand to curl around my stomach.

Hope blossoms and the need to see Bash takes over.

"What are we going to—"

"Tilly! Thank god." Vivienne bursts through the drawing room door, hair falling wildly around her face. "It's Bash. And Cass. God. They are idiots—"

Eleanor stands at once, sweeping across the room to calm Vivi. I am closely behind and my best friend curls over, catching her breath.

"Freddy found me but he couldn't come. He is searching for a doctor to be there."

"Be where, Vivi?" I am confused.

"They were at the club, drinking, and Cassius made some comment about Sinclair, and you, and Bash. Sinclair heard it. They got into a fight. Bash challenged him to a bloody duel. Sinclair agreed and told him that if Bash kills him then you are free. That he can have you."

"That's ... but ... duelling is illegal," I stammer. My heart thunders in my chest, my blood pulses so loudly in my ears it makes my head hurt and my throat constrict.

"I know that. Freddy is going to find a doctor, but ... Tilly, Sinclair is not a gentleman. They will not settle this like gentlemen do. He will not shoot at the sky," Vivienne says.

The baby boy with his messy black hair and nose that's identical to Bash's disappears from my head. It is replaced cruelly with the image of the man I love with a pistol in hand, a hole in his body, and the life draining from his eyes.

I shudder, my stomach churning again and bile moving dangerously up my throat.

"Where, Vivienne?" Eleanor snaps. Her voice cuts through my thoughts, blurring the picture of a dead Bash and bringing me back to the drawing room.

"The park. Just before sunset."

"I— I don't ..." I shake my head.

"Matilda. My dear." Eleanor takes my hands again, her gaze steady as she holds my eyes. "You must go with Vivienne and stop this. Tell Bash about Sinclair and Ravenswood. Tell him it's over and send Sinclair back to his parents. I will go to your mother and father. I will handle the rest."

I can only nod, collecting my shoes from their discarded spot on the floor and racing after Vivienne.

The carriage seems to roll through the streets at a snail's pace, the thundering of my heart causing my head to pound. I try a few deep breaths, needing to clear my head so I can figure out what to say when I see him.

"What did Eleanor mean? Why is it over? What happened to Sinclair?" Vivi asks, sitting across from me as the carriage rattles across the city.

I glance at her to see the curiosity written all over my friend's face. My eyes go back to the small window, watching the houses blur by as I say, "He got Charlotte Ravenswood pregnant."

"Christ." Vivi swears under her breath. "Isn't Charlotte engaged to a Prince?"

"I do not care." I shrug and it makes Vivi tut. I turn back to face her. "What if Bash dies, Vivi? What do I do then?"

"He won't. He won't die." Vivi shakes her head.

"What if he does?"

Vivienne doesn't have time to answer me.

The carriage rolls to a stop and I practically fall from it, stumbling as I step onto the grass. The sun is low amongst the trees and darkness settles around us. Vivienne stands by my side, listening with me, and just as I start to feel the bile rise in my throat again—because it is just so quiet—we hear the shouting.

Hearing his indistinguishable voice echoing through the quiet as if it were a pin and the air a balloon, causes my heart to jump and skip a beat.

"Tilly—"

I take off.

Lifting the hem of my dress, I run through the grass and toward the voices. The trees begin to thin and I weave through them, waiting to be close enough to call out his name.

To stop this.

But as I make it to the clearing the pair are already finishing their last steps.

Their pistols aim at the sky.

Freddy hears me first, his head turning and his eyes widening when I yell. He moves, just as Bash and Elliott turn. There follows a swift shift of limbs and a shot rings through the air. The birds rustle into flight from the trees. The smoke from the pistol lifts away in the wind and the silence engulfs me once again.

And then a scream rips through me. Wrenching from my lungs, it blisters my throat. Freddy catches me by the waist as I try to propel myself closer to the body lying in the grass. He pulls me to him, capturing me, as my eyes sting and I see red.

The image of the baby boy—with his messy hair and his button-like nose—comes forth and fades.

The house in the country that is quiet just before the sun rises as he wakes me with his lips seems distant and lost.

The white dress, the perfect dress, sits crumpled on the floor. Heavy and unworn.

I never will, now. I swear it.

Chapter Nineteen
Bash

Red.

That's what I remember seeing moments before the smoke enveloped me, the pain shot through me and black dots burst behind my eyes.

Just, red.

I've always liked the colour; specifically the shade that often changed depending on how the sun hit it or when it was still damp from the rain. I love it when it is tied into a bun, or falls loose over her shoulders, highlighting the pearly, porcelain skin I've spent hours committing to memory.

The sun bares down too brightly, too hot on my skin, and I feel too light. The surface of the pond shimmers and the trees edging the small woodland sway. Yet I can't feel the breeze where I stand. I touch a hand to my left side, where I remember the pain emanating from not moments ago but there is no mark or blemish that could explain what might cause it. Something is off. This feels ... nothing is right here.

Wherever here is.

"Bash?"

My neck snaps around searching desperately for the source, for the girl that owns that voice. For Tilly.

"Bash, can you hear me?"

My reply gets lost in my throat, turning into a groan that merely falls in silent frustration. I can't call out to her. Can't reply. The air in my lungs is heavy and unmoving so I focus inwards. I have no heartbeat, no familiar thud in my chest, no skip or jump that I have come to expect whenever I hear her voice.

There is only silence.

"Bash ...please ...don't leave me."

I shut my eyes, blocking out the much too bright sun and the soft grass beneath my feet. Tilly. She is somewhere—not here, that is obvious—but somewhere and she needs me. There is a plea in her voice, a waver in her ordinarily strong conviction, a soft prayer when she whispered my name as it floated across the non-existent breeze.

Yet I can only stand and wait and listen in the silence that surrounds me.

I remember standing in the park in London with Cassius at my shoulder and Sinclair down the barrel of my pistol.

I remember thinking that it is much easier to die when you are dying for love.

The shot rang out and I thought of her.

The setting sun is a fitting background to the final moments of my life since it has become my most favourite time of day.

With the setting of the sun comes Tilly.

The warmth of her bed and the feel of her body against mine, and the sound of her whispers and whimpers as I show her just how much I love her.

Sinclair didn't aim for the sky and neither did I. Both of us were dedicated to our mission up until the very last moment and, as I stand in the breezeless meadow with the impossibly blue pond, I pray that my bullet found its mark just as Sinclair's had.

"*Bash.*"

Another whisper.

Another broken prayer.

Her voice seeps into my skin and cools the blistering heat under the too bright sun. I picture her; the red hair that is a thousand different shades in one and the bright smile that pulls across her pink lips that I discovered fit perfectly against mine, and the wondrously smooth skin that I love to trace light patterns into as it glows in the moonlight.

I close my eyes.

Standing alone in this in-between where the sun is too hot and the silence too loud, I pay attention to what I'm supposed to feel. Her face front and centre in my mind, I think about the way my heart skips every time she smiles. About how I can't help my own smile whenever she laughs. About how my body craves hers whenever she is close.

The world darkens behind my closed eyes. A chill spreads down my spine as I feel the whisper of a cool breeze over my skin. A change.

I look up as a harrowing rumble sounds, and then another.

Clouds roll in and with them lightning that lights up the darkest of nights, accompanied by window rattling claps of thunder. As I picture her and the clouds above block out the blistering heat, my chest expands and the breeze turns into a blistering gale, swirling around me.

My heart begins to beat loudly, competing with the sounds of the storm, desperately fighting to be heard over the raging thunder.

To find its way back to her.

Chapter Twenty

Tilly

"Did you hear about the wedding that happened on Sunday?"

"No? I thought it would not go ahead because—"

"It went ahead alright. I heard that the bride cried the whole way down the aisle."

"God. That poor girl."

The Pembroke carriage sits motionless outside the Archibald's London residence. To anyone passing by it will seem empty, a lone footman sitting at the front as he waits for his employer. Two men stand close to the open carriage window and I have a front row seat to their idle chatter which is made entirely of gossip. They are close enough that the smoke from their lit cigarettes wafts lazily towards me on the gentle breeze, causing my throat to dry out and itch. I fight to suppress a cough.

I hate smoking. Hate how common it has become in London, that the clouds of smoke are almost everywhere I go. It makes me long for the country; fresh air, open spaces, private, and a world away from the society pages gossip writers.

I curl my fingers under the cuff of my dress and feel for the small handkerchief folded neatly against my wrist. I shake it out. My thumb traces the embroidered S and then the A before I press it to my mouth and nose, inhaling.

It still smells like him.

Just for a moment my eyes close and I see him. I see his smile, hear his laugh. It's like he calls to me, his hand stretching out to take mine before pulling me to him. I can almost feel his fingers trace my spine or press into my thighs or ghost across my collarbone as his lips search for my own.

I lift my hand to skim a gentle finger across my neck, mimicking the way Bash does it—*did* it—before he would kiss me.

I blink. A single, neat tear follows the well established path down my cheek. I don't bother to wipe it away. Every tear is proof of him, of us. Proof we loved. Proof Bash lived and that he was mine.

Every kiss, every touch.

I took it all for granted.

"You'd be distraught too. Engaged to a prince, married to a Sinclair." The voices filter into the carriage and my chest seems to ache with every word.

"Didn't he get her pregnant? I thought that's why it was so rushed?" one asks.

"Still, I suppose she hoped to play it off as the Prince's if a maid from Sinclair's household hadn't let it slip."

"Shame."

My face is entirely hidden. I have the plush velvet curtains bunched around the frame of the window to thank for that. Yet I can't help pulling my red hair over my shoulder and twisting it neatly out of the way, or pressing myself further into the corner of the carriage.

I want to escape. To fade away.

Without Bash, the gossip and the scandal feel too much. Too overwhelming.

It has been days since that fateful night. The one that lives on in my nightmares.

Cassius cradling Bash's almost lifeless body.

The blood stained grass.

The darkness fell, and Vivienne gently held me as Freddy and Cassius lifted Bash from the ground. I remember pleading with his limp body.

To stay with me. To fight. To stay alive.

They left and I have not seen them since.

Since then it has been a blur.

Vivienne brought me home Friday evening. She said nothing to my shocked mother, threw a glare at my father when he tried to demand answers and barked a sharp but kind order for Baggins to follow us upstairs.

I was covered in dirt and blood. My dress was filthy and ruined. Vivienne and Baggins stripped it from me and then burned it. They rinsed my hair and scrubbed the mud from my skin before I crawled into bed. I shudder as I think about the blurry memory. No one had told me if he lived but they also hadn't brought the news that he died, either.

When the morning light crept through a crack on the curtains covering my windows and the perfect, gorgeous white dress was illuminated, I finally cried.

I cried silent tears into my pillow and waited for my mother to wake me. Waited for Baggins to enter and gently guide me to my dressing chair so she could pin up my hair and put rouge on my cheeks. Waited for them to force me into the dress.

Then, down the aisle.

But nobody came and the sun set on my wedding day.

After that, I seemed to have lost count of the days. I slept for most of them. Bathed and ate a small amount before falling asleep again. Still, no one brought word of Bash and my heart continued to break.

This morning was different.

Vivienne fought through the lock on my doors and ripped back the curtains. She forced me from my self-imposed isolation. Without so much as a brush being run through my hair, Vivi pushed me into this very same carriage I sit in now, and we circled London.

Vivi chatted about nothing whilst I grew tired of the grey, stone buildings and the hum of the carriage rolling over cobblestone. It lured me into a restless sleep. My eyes itched and I was about to demand to be taken home when my gaze slid over the familiar blue door that I could see from my bedroom window.

We stopped at the Archibald house.

"Wait." Vivienne had clipped at me, stepping from the carriage and shutting the door firmly behind her.

So here I am, waiting. Staring at the blue door and still left wondering.

I twist my hair again, tightening the strands around my fingers, as I listen to the men gossip as if they are maids at the morning markets. I glance down at my hair against my pale fingers. The red has dulled since the day in the park.

As have the sun and the moon and all that makes the world turn because I had not been fast enough, not nearly enough, to get to him first.

"Good news for the Prescott girl. Can't believe she'd be unhappy with the outcome."

"Agreed. She dodged a bullet." The men wander away, their voices trailing after them with the wind. I let go of my hair, a few tears soaking into the handkerchief I still press against my mouth.

Elliot Sinclair walked down the aisle on Sunday, but with a different bride on his arm. He left with a silently crying Charlotte Ravenswood. A small gathering of waving family members saw them off on a honeymoon in the country that would extend for the next six months, only for them to return with a baby. Elliot Sinclair will continue to live his life as if nothing has happened.

Bash and I will continue to pay the higher price for our love. With blood, and grief, and our lives.

I flinch when the door to the carriage is thrown open. I fold the handkerchief into a closed fist. Vivienne watches me for a moment, her chest heaving as if out of breath before a smile flickers across her features.

I stare back, not a single word forming on my tongue as I blink at her.

"He is alive," she says.

A flicker of sunlight sparkles, reflecting in one of Vivienne's earrings. The flicker reflects around the carriage interior, pulling the vibrant colours from their dull shades as if bringing them back to life. The cigarette smoke, and the grief, and the inability to simply live without him lifts as my intense grief releases my heart from its clutches.

I find it unharmed, still beating heavily inside my chest. I lift a hand, wiping away a tear that sits stranded halfway down my cheek, the reminder that is no longer necessary.

"He's alive, and he's awake. He's asking for you."

Chapter Twenty One

Bash

"You look pale."

The words fall from her beautiful mouth as soon she opens the door. Laughter bubbles in my chest but I only manage to groan, the stitches in my side pull taut with her gentle humour. It is likely I do not look my best. Probably closer to death. I cannot bring myself to care. Not when I am looking at her.

In the dream, Tilly was the cool whisper that protected me from the blistering heat. Now I'm in my right mind, I rationalise that it must have been the fever taking over my body in the immediate days following the duel. I vaguely remember coming in and out of consciousness. The blurry memory of doctors rushing around my bed, and the desperate pleas of my mother to keep me alive sends shudders down my spine.

I'm thankful for those doctors, though. I always will be.

They brought me back to life.

Back to her.

Now here she is, fingers toying with a handkerchief, eyes red, lips swollen. Tilly is shaking and I can tell she's been crying. I can tell even with the distance between us. I wish I could spring from the bed, cross the room in a stride or two and take her in my arms.

I wish I could kiss her.

Here in reality, she is the light of a hundred sunlit days. A simple warm breeze swirling and heating my skin. She is my reason for fighting, for surviving, for living.

Her.

My Tilly.

"I think it might be one of the side effects of losing so much blood," I say but it only makes her sob—or laugh, I can't be sure—as her hand reaches up to cover her mouth. I wince as I pull myself up against the pillows, trying to look less like I am sitting at death's doorstep.

"I'm okay, Tils. I'm fine." I lift the light fabric covering my stomach, showing the twenty or so tight black stitches holding my skin together. "See?"

My attempt to calm and reassure her fails miserably. Her tears run freely over her flushed cheeks and the hand clutching the handkerchief trembles terribly.

"Fuck ... Tils ... will you come here? Please. I'm sorry." She takes a few uncertain steps, her knees bumping against the side of my mattress. "I'm okay. I promise."

"You ... Bash, he *shot* you."

"Yes, but—"

"No buts! He shot you. And, I—" She bites down on her bottom lip and the action goes straight to my groin. I know it's not the time. I am on bed rest and she has tears falling from her eyes. Yet my body is conditioned by her. To react and want.

To need her.

I can barely keep my hands off her in public let alone in a room, alone and with the door closed. Sometime soon, when the time is right, I will mention the subtle conditioning of my body's reaction to her presence. I want to tell her that she has me wrapped around her finger. It will make her laugh.

I love her laugh.

I bite down my grimace of pain and reach for her hand. She meets me in the middle. Our fingers entwine easily slipping into place as if they are missing puzzle pieces finally found, completing something unfinished.

"Please do not cry," I whisper. The words come out broken and shaking but the thundering rhythm in my chest is a constant reminder that I am alive and okay and fighting another day. For her.

"I am okay," I promise.

She watches me, her eyes a deep forest of unreadable emotions and still glistening with fresh tears but when she nods, my chest expands and my shoulders slump back into the wall of pillows holding me up.

"Will it hurt if I ... sit?" She pulls her lip between her teeth again, her eyes questioning.

"Tilly ..." My eyes drop to the handkerchief in her hand. I recognise it as the one I left on her dressing table as I slipped from her bed before the sun had risen last Friday.

I did not sleep that night. I did not want to waste any of the limited time left with sleep. Instead, I had sat against Tilly's headboard and just stared at her.

Stared as her chest rose and fell. As her hair spilled over her shoulder, her lips parted just slightly. Every so often she would let out the smallest of sighs as she dreamed. I remember the way I'd almost stopped breathing the first time she did it and with the second, a small smile had crossed her lips as if she had been dreaming of something happy and uncomplicated.

I wished that I could dream with her.

I sat watching her until the very first whisper of the day appeared, the light barely peeking between the stone houses. Then I kissed her gently, drawing another of her delicious sighs and I left.

That evening I got shot.

"I'm sorry I scared you. I shouldn't have done it. It was—" I tug at her hand, our fingers still tangled together, wanting her to get closer.

I want to kiss her. So, so badly.

"Stupid," she finishes for me. "So stupid."

The corners of her mouth lift a little as she fists the fabric of her skirt to crawl onto the bed. She sits by my side with her legs tucked beneath her and our hands in her lap. My thumb gently rubs against hers and my racing heart calms a little with the contact.

"If you had just waited," Tilly sighs, tightening her grip on my hand. "If you had just come to me that night like you were supposed to, I would have told you that Elliot Sinclair got Charlotte Ravenswood pregnant with child."

"So you did not …?" Did I hear her right? She doesn't look up, her gaze set firmly on our entwined hands.

"They got married on Sunday morning. Quickly and quietly," she says. I wish she would look at me. "Every maid or footman in London knew by Saturday morning about her and by the evening you taking a bullet in a duel was old news. Her father is furious with Lord Sinclair."

I squeeze her hand. "Prescott, look at me."

She scoffs at the use of her last name, a laugh bubbling up and mixing in with her sobs. The pain in my side suddenly seems unimportant. I lean forward, wincing but gritting my teeth until I am mere inches from her. "This is good, isn't it?"

"Well, horrid for her … she was engaged to a prince after all … but for us. Yes, it's good," she sniffs.

"So why are you still crying?" I ignore the painful throbbing in my stomach and edge closer to her.

"I almost lost you." It is a whisper that drops from her lips in a soft sigh. I remove my hand from her lap, pushing her hair behind her ear before tracing along her jaw. When her eyes close under my touch I can't help but smile. I swallow my groan and lean forward.

I kiss her. Gently, softly. I prove to her that the blood in my veins still runs warm, that I live, and that time has changed sides.

Finally.

"I am right here," I tell her as my lips brush hers with the words. "I am right here and I will never, never, leave you again."

"Bash—"

"Will you get something for me? In the top drawer of my desk, just over there." My gaze flickers toward my desk.

I have stared at the small, velvet box too many times since purchasing it not to be able to see it clearly in my mind. Her brow crinkles, her mouth turning downward for a moment as she searches my face. Another soft smile moulds my lips and I kiss her again.

Time is on our side.

I run my thumb across her bottom lip, pulling from her another soft sigh as I ask, "Please?"

Annoyance flashes in her eyes, as if moving from her spot is an effort she would rather not make. I rather she does not move either but, again, the small velvet box crosses my mind and I find myself almost wanting to push her from the bed.

When she gets up, I can't help watching the swing of her hips as she crosses the room. While I'm sure she exaggerates her movements, the wink thrown over her shoulder is very telling, I appreciate the view nonetheless. She tuts at my messy desk, loose parchment and books spilling across it with little order.

"I cannot imagine how you expect to get anything done ... such a mess." Tilly starts to shuffle the parchment into order, the books into piles.

"I have an office that I work from," I remind her.

"One that I am sure is just as horrendous. You work with Cassius and he is likely to be just the same." The clicks of her tongue and breathless head shakes go on but as they do so, my nerves prickle further under my skin.

"Tilly, the top drawer."

"Yes. In a minute, I just want to put these in—"

"Prescott, will you just—"

"Fine, fine. You do not have to Prescott me—"

A knock at the door interrupts her and Tilly jumps, hand going to her chest. My mother lets herself into the room. She looks between Tilly, standing next to my desk, and me on the bed looking surprised to find us so far apart.

"Sorry, I–" she takes a deep breath. "Tilly, dear. Your father is here to escort you home."

"Oh." Tilly glances at me.

"Mother, can you give us a moment?"

She raises her brows but nods sharply. "Yes, but I am leaving the door open. You both still have reputations to protect."

I hold back a laugh as Tilly goes white and furiously nods. My mother gives me a pointed look and leaves. The door stays wide open.

"I have to go," Tilly whispers, crossing the room and sitting back on the bed gently.

"Okay," I reply, taking her hand in one hand and lifting the other to trace her cheek.

"Should I come back tomorrow?"

"If you do not, I will be forced to come to you."

"Don't you dare," she whispers, leaning in.

"So I will see you tomorrow then." I brush my lips against hers. "I love you, Tils."

"I love you too."

Tilly

I wake to the news that my mother has left for Paris. Father stops me on my way out the door to pass on the message that she received an urgent message from a cousin and left before the sun was up. I take the message without looking at my father and leave the house, crossing the cobblestone street without looking back.

Bash is in the drawing room when the footman leads me inside.

"I'm not going." Bash's voice carries from the open doorway. The footman enters ahead of me so he can announce my arrival to the family but I don't pause. He's halfway through saying my name when I round the corner to see Bash propped up against pillows on one of the love seats. Two doctors stand over him, Eleanor and Jonathan are by the windows, and Cassius lounges on a chaise across from him with his legs draped over Vivienne's lap. Freddy is in the armchair in the corner, a book on his lap.

"Sebastian. Watch your tone." Eleanor snaps. I don't miss the way she melts into Jonathan's touch when he gently tugs her toward him and rubs a hand down her arm.

"Mr Archibald, you have been shot. Country air and a quiet environment is important to your recovery. It is highly recommended–"

"I am not leaving the city." Bash says through gritted teeth. He looks away from the doctor, eyes catching on me and his sharp expression softens.

"Hi Tils," he says. Everyone follows his gaze and I shift under the attention.

"What is going on?" I ask.

"Sebastian will be travelling to Wescombe today. To recover." Jonathan states. His words are stern. Final. And with them, my heart shatters.

Away. To Wescombe. Their country estates.

No.

"I am not going." Bash's voice rings in my ears.

"You are. That is final," Jonathan says. "Thank you, doctor. We will have the carriage ready shortly. I have already sent a footman ahead to prepare the staff."

One by one, the doctors and Bash's parents file past me and out of the room.

Bash holds his hand out for me. I fall into his side gently and careful not to touch the bandages.

"Don't argue. It will only be for a few weeks," I say, pushing my hand through his hair softly.

"A few weeks away from you." Bash sighs, catching my hand and pulling it toward him. He runs his finger over my left hand, fiddling with fingers like he's looking for something. I turn my palm over and catch his wandering fingers.

"You left for years while at school. We managed," I remind him.

"We were twelve." He sounds like a toddler about to throw a tantrum. I smile. "Besides, that was before I saw you naked. Now knowing what's under all the dresses and the corsets—"

"You have been shot, Sebastian Archibald." I laugh, gently leaning into his shoulder. My fingers drop to brush over the bandages. "There won't be any of *that* until you fully recover."

He raises his brow at me, disbelief evident in the mischievous smirk that spreads across his lips.

"I mean it, Archibald."

He presses my open palm to his lips before continuing down and kissing my wrist.

"Fine." He fiddles with my fingers again. "Tell me again why you cannot just come with me?"

My heart flutters. The earnest longing in his request setting off butterflies to flutter around in my stomach and, even though I won't admit it to him right now, heat to build between my legs.

"It isn't proper."

"Vivienne can come too," Bash argues, voice growing a little louder, inviting back up for his argument.

"I cannot be a chaperone for Tilly when I still need one myself, Archibald. Christ." Vivienne and Cassius seem to have swapped and she now leans against his chest with his arms encasing her. "It is a few weeks. You will be fine without her."

Bash mumbles under his breath, face dropping to my shoulder, hiding amongst my hair as he presses his lips to the small spot beneath my ear. I jolt, my face heating, as I feel him suck gently at my skin. I bite down on the inside of my cheek and tug gently at the nape of his neck. He pulls back, the smirk and the mischief still well and truly present.

"She's right, you know." I run a hand through his hair, smoothing it down as best I can. "You will be fine without me for a little while. It'll be better, this way, you know. By the time you're back, the shooting and the scandal with Elliot will be long forgotten."

"I don't—"

"This town is full of gossiping Mama's and I would rather not have people spreading rumours that we are doing anything untoward," I whisper, "Poor Charlotte's reputation is ruined ... not that I feel all that bad for her but still ... "

"We are doing untoward things, though. Lots of them ... we're good at them, too ..." He drops a kiss to my shoulder.

I pull in a sharp breath. "Stop it."

Bash pouts, looming terribly close to my neck again. If he doesn't relent sooner, I am bound to give in.

"Fine. I will go. But I will miss you terribly and I will not sleep a wink without you," he says quietly.

"Good." I smile, my heart skipping a few or more beats when he leans over and kisses me properly, stealing the air right from my lungs.

Tilly,

London disappears behind me, as do you. The only comfort I have is that I left my heart in your hands. Promise me you will keep it safe until we reunite. I will be counting the days.

Bash.

Bash,

London is dull without you. Father has stayed at his office and Mother has yet to return from Paris. She wrote just after your departure.

I miss you.

Vivienne said Cassius wrote and said you were being a bore.

Is it because you miss me too?

I attended the Dearborn Concert last night. Everyone stared.

I think I would be fine if you were here with me but I have become tired of the whispering of London society. They will not stop staring at me. Whether it is about Elliot and Charlotte or the duel, I do not know. What I would give to be there with you, a bore or not, in the quiet of the country.

I am counting the days as well.

Tilly.

Tilly,

I miss you.

Terribly.

How could I not? I hate being apart from you, I have always hated being apart from you. I will not lie, the country has been nice and I cannot say I am envious of the staring and the whispering even if hearing that it's happening makes my blood boil.

I am so sorry, my love.

One day soon I will whisk you away and keep you hidden in the countryside. All to myself.

Know that I think of you. Head held high, my love. You are not the one ruined by a pregnancy to a man whom you were not even engaged to, even if we had toed the line ourselves for a moment. I promise to make it up to you as soon as I see you.

Come to Wescombe.

I love you,

Bash.

P.s. Cass is an arse. Ignore any further messages he tries to pass through Vivienne.

Bash,

I cannot sleep without you.

I love you,

Tilly.

Tilly,

Open your curtains and look at the moon. Know that I look at
the same one.

Dream of me, my love.

Bash.

Bash,

Cassius tells me you have been badgering your doctors. He writes that you're hurrying them along and demanding they take out your stitches before they are ready. Stop it. I swear if I find out you've done anything to prolong the healing process because you've been reckless with the doctors' instructions, I will personally come down there and ensure you remain on bed rest. And no, before you get any ideas, there will be no joining you in said bed.

Listen to your doctors, please.

I cannot bear the thought that we could remain apart longer than needed.

Thinking of you,

Tilly.

Tilly,

I will be killing Cassius.

Will you write to me when I go to prison?

Bash.

Bash,
You are being dramatic.
Tilly.

Tilly,

I swear, I've not slept a wink and my heart stopped beating the moment I lost sight of London. You call me dramatic but you've made me this way. Loving you is like breathing air. I need you to survive.

How has it been five weeks?

I'm afraid I may never sleep again and if I never sleep again, I will never dream of you. I yearn for darkness to fall now, so that I may lay in bed and think of you. I dwell on those quiet moments that I had you in my arms. I miss your voice. I miss those little noises you make when we are alone and I can kiss that one spot beneath your ear. My sheets are too cold and too empty without you next to me. I want to keep you in bed until I've counted every single freckle imprinted on your soft skin, I don't think I ever have. I long to see you, to touch you, to kiss you.

Come to Wescombe.

Awaiting your arrival,

Bash.

Bash,

I am missing you more and more with each day. I turn over in bed and expect you to be there. The thoughts of a future that is now ahead for us brings more than a smile to my lips. I think of your touch and the nights spent in bed with you.

Maybe when we reunite and just for a little while, we might hide away in bed. Do you think we could find somewhere to hide from the world before we have to start making decisions and being proper members of society? I think I might need that. It is not very proper but I have begun not to care very much about being proper. It is hard without you here.

For now, I will remember the feel of your lips on mine and wait for the real thing.

Promise to never leave me for this long ever, ever again.

Sleep, so you can visit me in your dreams as I do you in mine.

Your love,

Tilly.

Tilly,

You underestimate my creativity. This house is very large, with hundreds of rooms. Many in a hidden alcove and shadowy corners. Bed is not the only place I plan to distract you from society dramas, I promise you that. Wait until I have you in my arms again. Perhaps I will make it my mission.

Six weeks is much too long.

Have you heard from your mother? Freddy will come to London to bring you to Wescombe. Pack a bag. Tell Baggins, or your father, or whoever you please. Just get in the carriage and come to Wescombe. Don't think about it. Just get in the carriage. I need to see you.

Write that you will?

Bash.

Chapter Twenty Two

Bash

"I am impressed, Master Archibald. You've healed very well."

I grin as I watch the doctor remove the white bandage for the final time. The scar that runs down my stomach and skims my hip is a light pink. It will fade but it will still likely last forever. Cassius keeps telling me that scars make a man desirable. I am yet to believe him.

As my stitches get removed and the wound closes over, my only thought is on Tilly. On the fact that she won't have that small crease in her forehead or a mask of concern all over her beautiful face.

The scar can linger as long as I get my future with Matilda Prescott as the result.

She has consumed my thoughts completely from the moment I left her in London. Not that she doesn't completely consume me when we are together, but at least then I am able to kiss her, to touch her, and settle any type of desire building in my chest within a few hours.

Being apart from her has the desire just building ... and building ... and building.

I long to see her. To talk to her, to touch her again, to reacquaint myself with her body.

"Bash?" Cassius knocks me on the underside of my head, getting my attention and giving me the beginnings of a headache. He is looking at me with raised brows and an amused smirk. He nods his head, directing me to turn.

"What?" I ask. My eyes follow Cassius' nod to the door of the drawing room where Nora stands waiting. "Sorry Nora. I missed what you said?"

"The post has arrived."

Tilly. A letter from Tilly.

"Any—"

"You may want to come outside, sir." She turns on her heel and walks away.

I glance at Cass, who is still staring curiously at the open door Nora vacated. My friend meets my gaze and shrugs. I look over at the doctor, who also shrugs and begins packing away his instruments.

"Light activity for a few more weeks." The doctor lifts his bag from the floor. "I mean that Sebastian. I do not want to be back here next week because you've ruptured something."

The doctor eyes me as I stand, tucking my shirt back into my trousers. "Promise, doc. I've got a fairly decent incentive," I say, thinking only of soft lips and quiet whimpers, hands twisting amongst red hair and her body pressing against my own.

I follow both the doctor and Cassius out of the room, itching to find whichever footman is withholding my letter from me.

I asked her to come. Demanded, really.

I've already made Freddy pack for London while we await her reply. Our letters only take a day or two to reach one another but it is far too long for my liking. I expected her reply days ago.

I miss her more than any other time in my life. Even when I was at school and distracted with schoolwork and my newly found knack for mischief, I missed her. That is nothing compared to now.

I can barely function without her. Sleeping is near impossible. Breathing even harder.

I should have insisted she come with me. Forced her into the carriage if necessary.

It is not as if the gossip about us could get any worse.

Tilly hadn't wanted to give them the chance, but from what she has written, it hasn't mattered. They gossip and whisper and laugh behind their hands at her expense. Her efforts have been fruitless.

If I had just insisted, she could be here with me, hiding away from all of that.

Instead she is in London and alone.

Laughter floats in from outside as Cassius and I make our way through the foyer toward the front doors of the house. Freddy appears in the open doorway, blocking my view of the commotion happening on the steps outside.

"Fred, what's—"

More laughter rings out. It makes my heart skip. The sound is beautiful and harmonious. Something like anticipation buzzes beneath my skin and I almost trip over my own feet as I practically run for the doors. Freddy grins before stepping aside, clearing the path for me to see down the front steps of Wescombe.

With baggage being unloaded by a flushed footman and a flustered Mrs Baggins, Tilly stands at the bottom of the stairs with a grin on her face and her eyes squinting in the sunlight.

My Tilly.

Her smile only brightens when her gaze lands on me. I match her, grinning widely.

My heart starts to beat in my chest again. My lungs fill with air.

I can breathe again.

Cassius' bark of a laugh echoes as he claps a hand against my shoulder before he takes the steps two at a time to wrap Vivienne in his arms when she climbs out of the carriage. Mrs Precott follows her.

The doctor follows me down the front steps, introducing himself to the newcomers before bowing his hat to us all and making his way toward the large gates at the end of the front road and back toward the village.

I begged. I demanded. I wished for her to come to me. To join me in the countryside.

Here she is. A picturesque illusion of sunshine and happiness. Smiling, and laughing, and standing right in front of me. *Please let her be real.*

I drink her in, my eyes darting over every inch of her body.

Red hair. Porcelain skin. Soft blue dress. Deep forest green eyes.

The hollow look that haunted her face the moment she opened my door all those weeks ago to see me sitting in bed, barely alive, is gone. The dark circles beneath her eyes are gone. Her face is bright, her cheeks have their regular pink tinge and her eyes sparkle.

Utterly perfect, healthy, and *here*.

I reach for her waist, my hands slipping around her body and pulling her into me. I inhale her perfume. My face drops into her neck as her fingers scrape up my neck and into my hair. I tighten my grip and her feet lift from the ground. Toes skim gravel and her laughter is loud and infectious in my ear as I spin us.

I place her back on her feet. Fingers trace full, flushed cheeks. Eyes gaze over the little, missable features of her face; the pattern of her freckles, the shallow dimple of only one of her cheeks when she smiles, the perfect curve of her cupid's bow. The gold flecks in her eyes sparkle in the sunlight, her iris' flashing every shade of green as she blinks. My heart thuds in my chest, my body humming in approval at her proximity.

"I missed you," she says.

I kiss her, slowly and gently.

My hands frame her face and I sigh into her mouth.

Home.

Kissing her is like coming home. After weeks apart my mind, my body, my soul has ached from missing her. But as her lips part, just a little, and I get a taste of her again the ache in my chest subsides. Calm and content.

Someone clears their throat and Tilly jerks back as if she forgot where we are and who stands around us. I look over to Freddy. His fist covers his mouth as he coughs again and raises a brow, a smirk lifting his lips.

"I think we might just ... Catherine, would you like some tea?" my mother says, turning her back to Tilly and I as she motions for Catherine to follow her into the house. Tilly leans into me and hides her face in my chest. She is bright red. I thread my hands through the loose strands of her hair and tuck her tightly into my side.

"I'm going to unpack. It has been a long day." Vivienne says. "Cassius, bring my bags will you?"

Cassius gives her a glare but collects her travel trunks anyway and follows behind her. Freddy only nods at me, following the other two up the stairs.

The fresh country air swirls around Tilly and I in a light breeze and the sun shines above, blue sky stretching for miles and not a cloud in sight.

"God, I missed you too. I did not think ... you did not write ... " Tilly leans back as I speak and I can't help but kiss her again.

"I meant to, but Mother came home and I begged to come see you. I did not think she would say yes but ... here we are," she murmurs, resting against my chest. I tighten my arms and keep her close. I drop my lips to her hair and inhale.

Sweet honey and fresh flowers. Her. All her.

She looks up at me with a smile forming on her face. Her thumb glides down my jawline before it ghosts across my bottom lip. I kiss the pad of her thumb and she blushes, a content sigh falling from her lips.

"How long are you staying?" I ask.

"As long as we want."

I let go of her and take a step back, pulling at her hands gently until she steps around and is facing me. Her green eyes shine as she squints a little from the sunlight. I brush a loose strand of hair from her face before I slip my hand into my pocket.

I search for the ring that has been with me since I left her in London all those weeks ago. The cool metal band finds my fingers easily and I sink down to one knee in front of Tilly.

"Bash ... Bash, what are you doing?" she asks, but by the way tears fill her eyes and she covers her mouth with a hand, she already knows what I'm doing.

I pull the ring out of my pocket and hold it up. The diamond glitters in the sunlight. I twist it a little, mesmerised by the prisms the sun creates as it hits the delicately cut edges.

"How about forever?"

Chapter Twenty Three

Tilly

"Yes!"

The word flies out of my mouth before he can even finish his sentence.

"Tilly," he laughs, getting up from his knee and holding the ring in front of me between two fingers. "I had a speech, a plan."

"Oh?"

"Will you let me ask you? Properly?"

His hazel eyes meet my emerald ones. My eyes flicker briefly up the stairs to the open front door where our families and friends disappeared through. I love them but for this, I would prefer to not have an audience. I want it to be Bash and I. Just the two of us.

Bash smiles, tucking a finger under my chin and bringing my attention back to his face, and his hand, and the ring.

"Matilda Prescott." The nerves pump through my body. I am acting as if I don't already know the question, as if we hadn't been painstakingly looking for a way to be together for weeks on end. I force myself to take a breath. "You were four years old when you came over and knocked down my block tower. You claimed you could build a better one—"

"I did," I interrupt.

He smirks, eyes narrowing playfully. "Sh."

I lean in and he meets me with a smile, taking a quick kiss before he brushes his thumb across my bottom lip. I nod for him to continue.

"You were ten when you told me that you should go off to school instead of me, because you were smarter. Twelve when you wrote to me about finally mastering archery. Fifteen when you complained that I needed more practice riding a horse because I couldn't keep up with you—"

"I could write a horse better than you. I still can," I interrupt him again. My fingers curl around the nape of his neck, burying themselves into his hair.

"I know." He smiles.

He kisses me again, and again. Small pecks against my lips until I smile and laugh when he presses his fingers into my side, teasing.

"You were saying?" I detach my mouth from his but don't retreat too far.

"Oh, right." He clears his throat, a mocking action that is supposed to separate our moment of laughter from the more serious moment of him asking to marry me. "Point is, I'd be stupid—more than stupid—to say that I could live without you. You are made for me, Tils, and I for you. Now that we have established that I'll do very dumb, very stupid, things to be with you, will you marry me?"

He twists the ring in front of my eyes a little, holding it up to the light. I wait a moment, holding back my smile and my answer. Unlike before, I let him blink and stare down at me as he waits for an answer.

"You promise to never challenge anyone to a duel ever again?" I ask.

"I promise," he replies with a nod.

"You swear to never do something as stupid and as reckless as putting yourself at the end of another pistol?"

"I swear."

"You'll never leave bed without waking me and telling me where you're going? And that you love me, first?"

"Never again."

"Then, yes."

"Yes?"

"*Yes.*"

I lunge forward, wrapping my arms around his neck and throwing my weight at his. He catches me. Of course he does. He always has.

Sebastian Archibald just asked me to marry him.

And I got to say *yes*.

My toes skim the gravel path again as he spins me in his arms, laughter filling my ears and happiness filling my heart.

"You make me so happy," he whispers as he sets me on my feet. "I love you."

I curl my fingers around his neck and tug his face towards mine. "I love you too."

Our lips meet again and I lose myself in his kiss. In his touch. His hands tighten around my waist and I feel my feet leave the ground again. As long as he doesn't stop kissing me, I don't care.

I gasp when Bash gently presses me against a stone wall. He's pulled me into a hidden alcove carved into the front steps. We are perfectly hidden. He buries a hand into my hair, tugging at the pins that keep it in place. It comes loose. He wraps the long strands around his fist twice and tugs lightly, forcing my face to his. He smiles.

"*Wife*," he says in an almost growl. "You are going to be my wife."

"Yours," I whimper against his lips as his free hand starts to grasp at the skirt of my dress, bunching it up. His fingers brush against the bare skin where my stockings finish and undergarments begin.

A finger brushes across my aching centre and I gasp.

"Finally," he says against my lips.

Before I can reply, he kisses me. It's wet, and hot, and raging. Almost as if he is trying to prove to himself that I am his now. No longer damned to be married to another, no longer bound by a contract that seemed so unbreakable.

I am his. And he is mine.

Finally.

"Bash," I whimper again as his lips drop to my neck. His mouth leaves a scorching trial as he moves down my neck, across my collarbone and over the soft peaks of my heaving breast. His fists bunch fabric, up and up until I can feel the gentle summer breeze on my exposed thighs.

I want him to tear my dress off. I want him to loosen this corset and replace the fabric with his touch. I need him.

Instead, he drops to his knees.

Fingertips slip across my waist and tug the silk fabric of my underwear down. Bash pulls them all the way down my legs and motions for me to step out of them. A confused question sits on the tip of my tongue before I swallow it, and the shocked gasp that crawls up my throat.

Bash's wet, hot tongue runs over my centre and I shiver. I lean back into the stone wall to stabilise myself as his mouth sucks and licks. His fingers dig into my thighs as I squirm above him. He groans, inching forward on his knees as his hand travels down my leg. He grasps the back of my knee and pulls it over his shoulder, securing me in place.

My hips rock in time with the rhythm of his tongue. My fingers thread through his hair. I'm likely going to make it more of a mess than it normally is but I cannot bring myself to care.

Not with Bash beneath me and his mouth on me like this.

A hitched gasp and a soft whimper when he slides a finger inside my body. I let out a loud, almost embarrassing, moan as my head falls against the stone and my eyes close. His fingers match his rhythm, drawing me closer and closer.

I fall over the edge of the cliff in mere moments.

He straightens my dress, not bothering to replace my underwear, but instead shoving the silk into his pocket. When he stands, I pull his lips to mine. I can taste myself on him but I do not care.

It isn't enough.

He chuckles, smoothing a hand over my hair and I realise that I must have spoken aloud.

"I have been without you for months now." He leans down and brushes another soft kiss against my lips. His hand finds mine and his fingers brush over the diamond sitting delicately on my finger. "I just had to touch you again. I missed you. So much."

"I missed you too," I whisper. I know the feeling. I do not think I have slept a full night since being away from him. I sleep best in his arms, with him wrapped around me and safe.

"It will never be enough, Tils. Not ever." He brushed a lock of hair from my face. "But soon you will be my wife. We no longer have to worry about any of that."

No. We do not.

Maybe as the years pass it might be. Maybe one day I will not feel this insatiable need to have his hands on my body or mine on his. But for now I want him. Again and Again. Over and over. His arm slips around my waist, his lips pressing into my hair, as he leads back around to the front steps of the house.

I melt into him, thinking about the timing of it all.

Time is no longer our enemy.

***

"You're engaged?" my mother practically screams as I hold up my left hand to show the room. Eleanor sits beside her, a cup of tea in her lap and a smile across her face. Harold folds the newspaper he is reading and drops it on the side table next to his seat.

"Fantastic news. Let's celebrate," he exclaims, making his way over to a small tray where a glass bottle of whiskey sits. He pours them out and hands a glass to Freddy and Cassius. Vivienne leans against Cass' chest on one of the sofas. Cass offers his glass to her and she takes a small sip before scrunching up her nose. He laughs, pressing his lips into the side of her head.

I smile at the pair of them, a small pool of guilt forming in my gut. In all my moaning and sadness about being apart from Bash, I forgot that Cass and Vivi were apart too. Separated from one another through no fault of their own but because they were being good friends to us.

"Congratulations," Harold says as he passes a glass to Bash. He bends, pressing a kiss to my cheek. When he pulls back, a warm smile has spread across his lips. "Welcome to the family, Matilda. I am so happy for you both."

"Thank you," I murmur, blush rising in my cheeks as Bash pulls me tighter to his side.

"So, when are we thinking?" Eleanor says, exchanging her tea for a glass of whiskey when it's offered to her.

"How quickly do you think they will give us a marriage licence?" Bash asks. He drags me over to one of the armchairs, sitting down before pulling me onto his lap. He wraps an arm around my waist so I can't protest.

"Sebastian," Eleanor rolls her eyes.

"What?"

"You are so dramatic." She takes a sip of her glass, tutting at her son. "Catherine and I will need time to plan a wedding. These things do not happen in a day."

"Actually," I say. "I would like to get married here. If you will allow it."

My mother's mouth opens, her eyebrows rising and a crease appearing between them.

"Here? At Wescombe?" Eleanor asks. She glances over at my mother, still staring at me.

"It is beautiful and I love the country." Bash's arm tightens around me. "I think it will be perfect."

Eleanor exchanges another look with my mother before a bright smile crosses her face.

"We would be delighted. You can have the ceremony in the church in the village and we can hold the wedding breakfast here at the house. I will let Michaels know."

"Sunset," Bash says as Eleanor rises from her seat.

"Sorry?"

"We should have a wedding dinner. Not breakfast. At sunset." Bash looks at me, his fingers moving to gently stroke another loose piece of hair from my face. "That's our favourite time of day."

"Sunset it is," my mother says. She rises from her seat to follow Eleanor, presumably to tell Michaels and Baggins about the wedding. But, before she leaves the room, she comes over to where Bash and I sit. She places a hand on my cheek and I lean into her warm touch. "I love you, Matilda. I am glad you are getting your happy ever after."

"Thank you, mother," I say quietly, giving her my most convincing smile, even though I can feel the tears prickling behind my eyes.

She stays there a moment, her hand on my cheek and her eyes on mine, before smiling and patting Bash on the shoulder. Then, she follows Eleanor from the room.

Conversation amongst Harold and our friends resume around us. Excitement about the wedding and catching up from the last weeks apart taking over the conversation. The bubble that often surrounds Bash and I descends.

I close my eyes, leaning against his chest.

There is nothing more in this world that I want than to begin my life with Bash. I want to walk down an aisle that he is at the end of. I want to curl my hair and rouge my cheeks for the day. I want to wear my dress.

The perfect dress.

The right man.

I want to celebrate with our friends and our families before we travel the world on our honeymoon. I want to lock ourselves in a bedroom and make up for lost time. I want to fill this house with children; half me, half Bash.

If it were up to me, I would marry him today.

I would have the second he kissed me in my father's study. Back when the light from a single candle had flickered shadows onto the walls and for the first time, we spoke freely of our feelings for one another and boldly of the rarest feeling of them all to find.

Of love.

I look back on the moment and realise that it hadn't really been monumental for me. It hadn't completely thrown me out of sorts. I loved Bash for years by then but as he had kissed me—his palms warming my face as he held me, careful as if he were afraid to break a moment too perfect to actually be real, with his fingers brushing along my neck— the world had shifted just a little. My heart began to beat a little faster, a little harder.

Like he brought me to life, changing my whole world into something that is easy, and comfortable, and ...

"Are you happy?" Bash asks quietly.

I look at him, the soft hazel of his eyes melting into gold as he stares right back. The months of anxiety and sadness fade away as if they never happened. Bash's eyes are my future—bright, shining, infinite—and it makes me smile.

"Deliriously so."

Epilogue

Bash

I miss my wife.

We agreed—*negotiated*—that the single long trip would be easier than the scattered, uncertain weeks or days away that normally came with owning one of the largest trading businesses in England. It didn't make it easier. Not for any of us.

Cassius was missing the early moments of his young daughter's existence, only two months old when we sailed for the continent. Vivienne wrote, of course. She described every moment down to how many curls were growing on the little girl's head, but I wonder if it perhaps made it worse.

Freddy was a bore this time around, too. He was moaning about missing the renovations on his new London house. I think it was less about the house and more about the woman he's been keeping a secret from us the last few months. I know there is someone because he insists there isn't. The miniature portrait he carries everywhere now proves me right.

Early on in the journey, there was a night when Cassius drowned his sorrows in the bottom of a bottle of whiskey. Freddy dragged him to bed. It left me wondering how I would do leaving Tilly behind if she were pregnant, or if we already had kids. Would I survive being away from them for so long?

Probably not.

Definitely not.

It is early morning when we reach home and Wescombe House finally comes into view from the carriage windows. As we cross the front doors and move slowly into the foyer, Freddy waves a tired hand before heading for the room he occupies when visiting. Cassius only grunts as he turns for the nursery, seeking out his daughter and Vivienne. Neither have returned to London since their daughter, Ava, was born. Tils and I don't mind. In fact, I think it would crush Tilly if Vivi left. They like having each other for company when Cass and I are away.

I think I will eat something, have a wash and sleep between the clean sheets of my bed. A bed that my wife will be in peacefully sleeping. I descend the stairs into the kitchens. Rubbing my hand over my tired face, I blink. The candles burn, flickering shadows along the walls.

Her hair is damp and her—no wait, *my*—robe brushes against the stone floor. She sits at the end of the long table, teapot still on the burner and a book in front of her. Her fingers toy with the edge of the pages. A loaf of bread, a knife, and a butter dish are laid out in front of her. I quietly watch as she turns a page of her book and reaches for a pre-torn piece of bread.

"A little early for breakfast?" I say quietly, unable to just watch any longer.

Tilly jumps, sucking air through her teeth, hand clutching at the fabric of the nightgown over her stomach. "God. Bash." She stands, her book forgotten on the table and her arms curling around herself.

"I'm sorry." I grin, drinking her in as I allow my gaze to fall over her. From her damp hair to bare feet. I move across the kitchen until my hands slide over her hips, up her waist, and around her. "Hi."

"You're home," she whispers. Her head drops to my shoulder and I press my nose into her hair, inhaling. She smells of roses and soap.

And a little of strawberries.

Her arms curl up around my neck, fingers burying into my messy hair as she pulls me down.

"Home. Finally," I murmur before capturing her lips with my own. I kiss her and the three months apart with pent up frustration and overworked bitterness and lack of sleep all melt away under her touch.

Never again.

We will find another way to secure the trade route and do business. I will hire someone else to take the trips if I have to. Three months apart is too long.

Never, ever again.

I whine a little pathetically when she pulls away from me and her fingers scrape along the nape of my neck. I'm not ready to let her go so I move my lips to her neck, to suck on the spot just below her ear that ...

"*Oh.*"

Makes her do that.

I smile when her breathing becomes a little rushed. My hands wander from her waist to curl over her hips. I intend to bury them between her thighs. Another breathless word—*Bash*—and I take a step back, pulling her with me. When the backs of my knees hit the bench seat, I sit. I curl my fingers into her thighs and slowly bunch the long night gown in clenched fists. I want, need to touch her bare skin.

I push the silk nightgown over her hips and she settles her thighs over mine. I slip the robe off her shoulders and let it fall to the floor in a heap. My hands continue to roam over her body, reacquainting themselves with her soft skin and delicious curves. My palms glide over her stomach, my thumbs brush the underside of her breasts. She gasps when I roll a thumb over one of her nipples and her back arches, pushing her chest out. She smiles as I gently kiss along her jaw. Her hands slip over my shoulders and her fingers spread against the back of my neck.

"I have to tell you something," she whispers.

I lean forward, mouth seeking hers but she evades me.

I pout but change course. I settle for the exposed trail from the sweet spot beneath her ear to the tops of her breasts. They rise and fall heavily as Tilly tries to steady her breathing under my touch. I reach the top of her nightgown, hands sliding the thin strap down her shoulder so the light fabric that previously created a barrier between my mouth and her skin is no longer a problem.

My tongue swirls around her nipple and she gasps, fingers twisting in my hair.

"So sensitive," I murmur against her. She giggles, her palms pressing against my shoulders and pushing me away gently.

I groan, "No."

"I have to tell you something. It cannot wait," she laughs again as I huff. I tighten my grip on her waist and pull her tighter against my chest.

"It has been months, Tils. *Months,*" I whine. "I want to fuck my wife. Then, we can talk. Please?"

She shakes her head, eyes sparkling with happiness even as they roll. She takes my hand, bringing it to her stomach and flattening my palm while covering it with her own. My thumb immediately begins a gentle back and forth motion. She drops her forehead to mine and sighs.

"You were about to have your way with me on the same table that Mrs Baggins eats from. She would be mortified." A laugh rumbles deeply in my chest. I love having Baggins here. I do. But caring about whether or not the table where I was about to fuck my wife is the same one Baggins eats at? Not at the top of my list right this second.

It's been a long, drawn out three months apart. Three whole months.

I would have had her in the entrance hall if we crossed paths there first. I always want her. Could be because I am madly in love with her. Probably is. But, I am also aware that it's an obsession. One I don't feel like trying to douse.

Thankfully, it is an obsession she shares for me too.

I think about telling her that. *Yes, my love*, I could say, *and Baggins will just have to deal with it.*

Instead, I just laugh.

"Can I ask you something?" she says. When I look up into her face I frown again, my hand still caught between hers and her stomach.

"You look worried."

"No, not worried." She shakes her head, adjusting herself on my lap. "Nervous."

"Nervous?"

"I like … " A familiar flush appears, creeping up her neck and it makes the concern rise in my chest. She's embarrassed.

Why is she embarrassed?

"I just mean, well, we like to have a lot of sex." The words spill out of her so fast I almost mishear.

"Yes. Is that a bad thing?" I continue gently rubbing my thumb against her soft stomach.

"No," she says. She smiles fondly, like a memory she often calls on for comfort comes to the front of her mind. Warmth spreads through my chest.

She is thinking of me. Of us.

"I just mean … will you still want me this much when I'm all pudgy and fat and grumpy? You know, when I am pregnant?"

I pause the hand slowly sliding up the outside of her thigh and my hand twitches against her warm, soft skin. "What kind of … obviously. I will always want you. Tils, what is—"

Oh.

Oh.

"Love ... " The hands covering mine on her stomach move to my shoulders. She uses them to help balance herself as she slips off my lap. My previous wandering hand shoots to join the other on her stomach.

When I really feel for it the tiny bump is obvious.

The strawberries. The sensitivity.

She hates strawberries. For as long as I've known her, she's never liked them. And she's always been reactive but not like that.

"The strawberries?" I whisper, edging closer to her on the seat. I can smell it on her breath, taste it on her tongue. Strawberry jam on bread.

"Cravings," she whispers. She drops a kiss into my hair, resting for a moment before continuing, "Remember when—"

"Yes. So you're ... ?" I inhale, drawing myself back to catch her gaze. "Mrs Archibald, are you pregnant?"

She smiles, exhales, tightens her grip on my shoulders, and finally nods.

Oh. My God.

She is gazing at my hands, or her stomach, or both.

But when she looks back up at me, her eyes glisten with tears. The confirmation sparkles in her bright green eyes. My heart skips and stutters, falling into an uneven rhythm as I surge upward, standing, mouth covering hers as quickly as I can. I swallow her laughter. Her body presses against my own. My hands are everywhere, again, and the kiss is deep, and messy, and passionate.

She's pregnant.

Oh my God, she's pregnant.

I sit back onto the bench, pulling her to stand between my legs. My forehead drops to rest on her stomach. Just above the small bump.

There was a time in our love story when I thought she was destined to be a fleeting part of my life. That I had waited too long on the edges of the ballrooms that ruled over our lives or hid behind our friendship and the letters I wrote to her in those vital, formative years.

There was a time, back when time hadn't been on our side and we had learned of our love for one another too little too late, that I thought I might never end up here. I thought that by some cruel path taken, some misstep, I missed my chance to love her and be loved by her.

My hands splay over her stomach, silently thanking whoever convinced time to switch to our side and I close my eyes. I remember the moments before I kissed her for the first time and how my world had been shadowed, waiting for her to come along and light my way forward—

"Hi." The words are breathless and my lips ghost over the small swell. "I'm Bash. Your father."

A misstep of fate or, perhaps, exactly the right one.

THE END

Acknowledgements

THE SECOND BOOK WAS scarier to release than the first. Thank you so much for taking a chance and reading A Misstep Of Fate! It is a story that formed a long while ago but has come alive over the last months.

My family and friends will always be thanked because without them, I would not be able to keep doing this. It's not for the weak and they lift me up every single day. They listen to me ramble, they ask endless questions and take an interest, and they celebrate all the wins regardless how little.

A special thank you to one of my best friends and my editor for this story, Giorgie. You are busy with your life and your career and your own real life book boyfriend but you made time for me anyway. I will forever be grateful. I love you so much.

To Bec. I would not have been able to do this and get A Misstep of Fate to where it is today without you. Thank you so much for the endless support, listening to me rant and rave, keeping me on track and just being the best over the last months. I am so grateful.

And finally to you, my readers. Once again, none of this would have been possible without you taking a chance on me and picking up the book. Whether you read PTLC and loved it or this is the first work of mine you are reading, thank you. You make this dream of mine worth chasing every single day.

About the Author

OLIVIA IS A ROMANCE indie author living on the east coast of Australia with her miniature spoodle, Scotland.

She's been writing since high school and is doing her best to live out her dreams of being a published author. Her hobbies are snuggling with her dog, reading all sorts of romance books, and hanging out with her family.

OTHER TITLES

The Boston Broncos Series
Play The Last Card
Play The Last Track

Standalones
A Misstep Of Fate